SORCERER

COVEN: BOOK 5

DAVID NETH

DN Publishing

Sorcerer
Coven, Book 5
Copyright © 2021 by David Neth
Batavia, NY

www.DavidNethBooks.com

ISBN: 978-1-945336-16-4
First Edition

Subscribe to the author's newsletter for updates and exclusive content:
DavidNethBooks.com/Newsletter

Follow the author at:
www.facebook.com/DavidNethBooks

ALSO BY DAVID NETH

COVEN
HARPY
SIREN
VALKYRIE
SHAPESHIFTER
SORCERER
WITCH (SHORT STORY)
ENCHANTRESS
ORACLE

UNDER THE MOON
THE FULL MOON
THE HARVEST MOON
THE BLOOD MOON
THE CRESCENT MOON
THE BLUE MOON

THE ART OF MAGIC

FUSE
ORIGIN
OMERTÁ
OBLIVION

HEAT
BLACK MAGNET
DUST STORM
THE GATEKEEPER

STANDALONE
ALL I EVER WANTED

CHAPTER 1

- JANUARY 1989 -

Freshly fallen snow covered the wooded landscape, untouched by mankind after the previous night's snowfall. In the Allegheny National Forest, there were very few people around to even disturb anything, especially so early in the morning.

But a sudden burst of bright light followed by a loud crack changed all of that as Ezra appeared. His hardy boots landed heavy in the snow. He pulled his fur coat tighter around himself and took only a fraction of a second to take in his surroundings before running off amidst the trees.

A moment later, another burst of light and an equally deafening crack sounded and Augustus appeared. Under the brim of his knit hat, his eyes darted through the early dawn darkness before he spotted his brother. Despite the many layers he was wearing and the freshly fallen snow, his pursuit of Ezra wasn't impaired.

"You run, baby brother, because you know you aren't strong enough to face me," Augustus grunted as he continued the chase.

He raced through the leafless trees, dodging downed logs, boulders, and frozen puddles. As he approached a slope, he shifted his body weight and slid down the snow. He took a heavy step once he reached the bottom and continued running. He only stopped when a long wooden staff extended from behind a tree and crashed into his skull, knocking him to the ground.

The being he had been chasing faded out with a burst of light and Ezra stepped into view.

Astral projection.

"Work smarter, not harder," he said.

Grunting, Augustus got to his feet and pointed his own wooden staff at Ezra, sending a streak of lightning soaring through the air toward him. Ezra rocked his shoulder back as he took the hit, firing his own burst of energy at Augustus.

The two traded attacks with one another, ducking behind trees and diving to the snow to avoid hits. Augustus, however, was more skilled. While Ezra took more time to summon stronger attacks, Augustus muttered ancient spells to himself to empower his own magic, creating a force field around his brother that sent Ezra's magic ricocheting back to him and knocking him to the ground.

Augustus approached and kicked away Ezra's staff—the channel for his magic—and stepped on his brother's chest.

"Where's the book, Ezra?"

Despite being overpowered, the younger brother smiled. "You may have stolen more powers, but without the book, you will never be as powerful as me."

Augustus pressed his boot harder against Ezra's chest. "Unless you're able to read the spells from the book, you're not so powerful yourself."

"But if you kill me, you'll never know where our family grimoire is."

"You stole it!" Augustus bellowed. "Tradition says that it goes to the oldest son, which you are not!"

Ezra smiled wide. "Oldest, no. But smartest, perhaps."

"Where is the book!"

Laughing, Ezra said, "I've hidden it so well that you will never find it. Killing me will make sure of it. And I know you're considering it, despite growing up side-by-side as best *friends*. After all, if I were in your shoes, that's what I would do."

Augustus rested his staff on Ezra's throat. "One last chance, brother. Where is the book?"

Ezra looked down and Augustus turned briefly to see who might've followed them. The distraction was enough for Ezra to grab ahold of the end of Augustus's staff and jam it up into his face when he turned back.

SORCERER

Ezra rolled across the snow and reached for his staff. It had landed between a fallen log and a boulder, wedged in just right so he couldn't reach it from his position on the ground.

Meanwhile, Augustus raised his staff above him and swirled it in the air. The wind picked up and the morning sky grew even darker as supernatural clouds rolled in. Soon, thunder followed. Waving the staff in Ezra's direction, Augustus summoned a bolt of lightning that struck down from the sky and connected directly with Ezra's chest.

Augustus watched as his brother's body lurched forward from the shock, then slammed back down onto the frozen ground. The clouds began to roll away as smoke wafted off of Ezra's charred, lifeless body.

Expectantly, Augustus extended his hand palm-out toward his brother's body. Slowly, a dim light extended from his palm to Ezra's heart as several sparks of light traveled from the corpse to Augustus.

When the transfer was complete, Augustus closed his palm and his eyes as he breathed in the addition of new powers. He might not have the family grimoire, but he had gained something from the outing. Even if he had to sacrifice his brother as collateral damage.

CHAPTER 2

Samantha's heart continued to race as she stepped into the Belle Valley Fire Hall. After all of their planning and preparation, she was less than twenty-four hours away from getting married.

And the lengthy to-do list weighed heavy on her mind.

Kathy and Steven laid out the tablecloths over the circular tables they had set up. Steven's mother, Mary, set out the small green tealight candles on each table, adorned with small solomon's seal flowers. The green candles represented love and solomon's seal root was used in hand fasting rituals, so Samantha thought a few of its flowers on the table would only help to give their marriage a little extra magical *oomph*.

Steven's father, Marty, and Steven's best man, Robert, were

pulling the round tables off the cart and setting them up for tomorrow's festivities.

"Nervous?" Talia asked Samantha.

Much to Mary's displeasure, Talia was going to be the officiant of the wedding. She sported black hair decorated with white beads, an assortment of rings on her fingers, three talismans hanging from her neck, and ripped black jeans under a faded green blouse that just barely covered the several tattoos along her arms.

Samantha and Kathy had found her at one of the herbal shops they frequented for their potion supplies. They hadn't confirmed that she was a witch too, but there was a definite possibility. There was an unspoken understanding between the sisters and Talia: they all recognized they were witches without verbally acknowledging it.

Samantha didn't mind whether or not Talia was a witch. She was more curious that the ceremony would be official, both legally and spiritually. Turns out Talia had it all covered.

Ever since Samantha introduced her as the officiant, Mary had been keeping her distance. Samantha assumed Marty or Steven had talked to her about it and told her to bite her tongue. It was too close to the wedding to cause waves and, if Samantha was being honest, she was smug about the fact that Samantha had come out triumphant with the wedding venue, among the other plans. While Samantha and Steven listened to Mary's input, they had the ultimate say about all of the arrangements.

And they didn't want much.

"Stressed is more like it," Samantha replied.

"These are all details," Talia assured her. "You've already done the hard part: finding someone to spend the rest of your life with."

Samantha sucked in a deep breath and let it out slowly. She'd been doing that more and more as a way to calm her nerves. "I know, but details are important too."

"To a degree. Is there anything else you want to go over about tomorrow?"

"No, it's not going to be that big of a crowd," Samantha said. "Steven really wants to do the whole, not-see-each-other-before-the-wedding thing." She rolled her eyes. "I guess I've planned everything else, so he can have that. We just have to make sure we're separated tomorrow."

"Steven told me he was arriving early tomorrow with his one lone groomsman," Talia said. "What time do you think you'll be arriving?"

Samantha looked over at Robert. Steven had wanted to invite a couple more of his friends from college. He'd been in their weddings, so it was assumed that they'd be in his too. But Samantha really only wanted Kathy standing up beside her. She didn't have too many other close girlfriends, so Steven decided to have only a best man to keep the wedding party small. She worried that he was compromising too much for her, but he assured her it didn't matter to him.

"I guess I'm going to make kind of a grand entrance tomorrow," Samantha told Talia. "Everyone should be here and seated already. Kathy and I won't come into the hall until we're about to begin. Then she'll walk out and we'll play the bridal march before I come out and make my grand entrance, I guess."

She wasn't a huge fan of being the center of attention, but she decided to soak up the moment for her wedding. It would bring memories for her to remember and maybe tell to her daughter one day, if she had one. Absently, she touched her stomach.

"Are you feeling okay?" Talia asked. "Nerves?"

Samantha nodded politely and waved Kathy over.

"Why don't I trade places with her?" Talia suggested and stepped over to help Steven lay out the tablecloths on the remaining tables.

Kathy walked over and flashed a bright smile. "This is exciting! It's actually happening!"

"Yeah," Samantha said without a hint of excitement in her voice. "You said the flowers are coming tomorrow morning?"

As a way to compromise with Mary on the venue, Samantha agreed to an outrageous number of flowers to freshen up the fire hall. Mary and Marty were footing the bill, so Samantha didn't mind. Besides, if she was being honest with herself, she knew the flowers *would* brighten up the drab space.

"Yup," Kathy said with a nod. "The florists are going to

bring them first thing in the morning so they're fresh. I've already explained to Steven, Robert, and Marty where we want everything to go. Cross your fingers that there aren't any hiccups. If worse comes to worst, they can always call us at the house."

"And we'll be at the house with the hairdressers?"

Again, Kathy nodded. "Yes. And the girl who is doing our makeup will be there at ten. By time either me or Mary gets done with our hair, we should be able to start right on makeup and then get into our dresses."

As a show of good faith, Samantha had also invited Mary to participate in a lot of the bridal party events. Not that there was much of a bridal party, but she could tell it made both Steven and Mary happy to see her making an effort.

"Oh no! The dresses! I was supposed to pick them up from the dry cleaners!" Samantha tucked her hair behind her ears.

"I already took care of it," Kathy said. "I took the bus to Steven's office downtown today and borrowed his car to pick up the dresses—and the tuxes. Everything is where it should be and it's all ready for tomorrow."

Samantha let out another deep breath. "Thanks, Kathy. I really appreciate it."

"Hey, being between semesters has given me time to get all of this running around done," Kathy said. She had just finished her first semester at Porreco College and was about to start her second in another week. "Good job picking a wedding date."

Samantha smirked. "Okay, here's another curveball: what about catering?"

"They're getting here around one. They're going to enter through the kitchen door so we shouldn't hear them at all." She turned and pointed to the counter with a window looking into the kitchen. "They're going to lay all the food out there, so when we're ready to eat, they should just lift the doors and we'll be on our way. It'll make clean-up for them easier too."

"Okay," Samantha said with a nod.

"Anything else you want to double check?"

Samantha's stomach rumbled. "Yeah, what about dinner tonight? I'm hungry."

"I ordered subs from a deli not too far from here," Kathy said. "I got you a turkey club, with light mayo, no pickles. Chip, from the fire department, offered to go get them for us about twenty minutes ago. He should be back anytime now."

Samantha smiled. "When did you get so responsible?"

"I'm just taking my maid of honor duties very seriously."

"Sam, do we have anymore of these candles?" Steven called from across the room. "I think we're one or two short."

"There should be another package of them in the bag I brought," she called back.

"Your purse?"

"No! Hold on." She walked across the room and pulled out a shopping bag from beneath her coat, which was laying on the stack of tables they hadn't used. "Here, I picked some up on my way over." She pointed to the carts that held the tables. "We're going to do something with these, right?"

"Chip said there's room to stash them in the storage closet," Marty told her. "We'll make this place look as best as it can be, don't you worry."

Mary scoffed as she laid out the last of the solomon's seal flowers, but Samantha ignored her.

The front door opened and sent a brisk chill through the room. Chip closed the door behind him and held up a plastic bag.

"Food's here!" he declared.

"Thanks for running out to get those." Samantha stepped toward him with her wallet in hand. "What do I owe you?"

"Don't worry about—"

Behind her, Mary let out a scream and Kathy called out, "Talia!"

Samantha spun around and saw the officiant writhing on the floor. Only the whites of her eyes showed and spittle foamed from her mouth. Robert sunk down beside her immediately and cradled her head.

"Call 9-1-1!" Samantha told Chip. He ran into the office.

Samantha stepped forward and watched as the woman she'd been talking to not ten minutes earlier was now having a full-on seizure on the floor. Selfishly, she hoped this wasn't a bad omen for what was to come.

CHAPTER 3

Cassandra bagged up an ounce of jasmine into a bag for Brittany, one of her regular customers. She didn't seem like someone who would come to an occult shop—from her bright blonde hair that smelled of hairspray to her limp wrist extended above where her purse sat at the crook of her elbow— but she was in once or twice a month getting an assortment of herbs. And she knew more than she let on about all the things in the shop. Cassandra had heard her help another customer when it was busy in the shop last October.

Meanwhile, another customer—someone completely new—perused the bookshelves at the back of the shop. He was a quiet-looking man with short-cropped hair and thick glasses. He kept his hands deep in the pockets of his thick winter coat as he read through the titles.

"Are you having trouble sleeping?" Cassandra asked Brittany as she tied a ribbon around the bag of herbs—silver ribbon, to bring peace and divinity.

"Yeah, I've been having nightmares," she said. "I'm hoping this will help me better than the drugs my doctor keeps trying to prescribe me. I just don't like taking a lot of pills, you know?"

Cassandra nodded and passed the bag to her. "Trust me, I know. Next time you make tea, add these leaves to the bottom of the strainer and run your hot water through for your tea. I promise you, it'll help you sleep."

Brittany smiled. "That was my plan. I've already tried some incense, but I don't want to do too much. I'm hoping this insomnia is temporary."

"Good luck and sleep well." Cassandra waved as Brittany exited the shop into the cold evening.

Turning, Cassandra sealed up the container where they kept the herbs and set it back under the register. As she pulled away, something appeared in a flash of light in the shelf beside the container.

It was a book—an old one. Leather-bound and scratched. The pages had yellowed with age and were all unevenly trimmed.

She stared at it a moment. Where had it come from? And why was it here?

The man by the bookshelves coughed and her eyes flickered

up to the last customer in the shop.

Crossing to the back of the store, Cassandra approached him. "Is there something I can help you with?"

He snapped around nervously, his face immediately going red. "Well, um…I don't know—I guess I'm just looking."

"Is there something in particular you're looking for?"

"It's stupid. My girlfriend is into astrology and I thought you might have something about it."

Her face lit up. "Oh, sure! We have a bunch of books about that. All down here on the bottom shelf." She stepped over to the second bookshelf and crouched down to pull out some options. "Is there something in particular she likes? Phases of the moon? Alignment of the planets? Constellations?

"Um…constellations, I think?" He sounded unsure. "She's really into signs and all that. She thinks her whole life was predetermined by the fact that she's a sagittarius."

Cassandra smiled and grabbed the book about constellations. "Ah, I see. This book explains the backgrounds behind those meanings and how the constellations were discovered and given meaning to. It's actually quite interesting and perhaps it's something you might want to take a look at for yourself."

He took the book from her but shook his head. "Nah, this isn't really my thing."

"But if it's something she enjoys, perhaps you owe it to her to see into her world a bit?"

He rocked his head back and forth. "I guess that's true. How much is this?"

She told him the price and he said he'd take it. She led him back to the register, where she immediately felt growing unease. The sudden appearance of that mysterious book didn't feel right, but she wanted the shop to be empty before she explored it.

The man paid for the book and Cassandra bagged it up for him and followed him to the door. Once he was back on the sidewalk, she flipped the "Open" sign over and locked the door.

Slowly, Cassandra retreated behind the counter again to inspect the book. It seemed to be radiating a dark presence and she was afraid to touch it, to even bump into it.

Grabbing a ceremonial cloth from the counter, she grabbed ahold of the thick tome and wrapped it tightly in the cloth, careful not to lay a finger on it. Carrying it to a back table where it was less likely to be touched, Cassandra took several careful steps away from it.

She let out a deep breath and gave a quick glance to the door before returning her attention to the book.

"Hurry home, Talia," she muttered to herself. "I have no idea what we've gotten ourselves into."

CHAPTER 4

Samantha sat in a chair at one of the tables they had set up for the wedding. She sucked in big breaths and let them out slowly, trying to prevent herself from having a panic attack. Meanwhile, the firehall remained frigid as the paramedics moved in and out of the open door to tend to Talia, who had thankfully stopped convulsing.

Steven sat beside his future wife and rubbed her back. Kathy sat on her other side and watched quietly as Talia was lifted onto a stretcher. Mary, Marty, and Robert all stood around solemnly and watched as the first responders worked. Mary had wrapped herself in her coat and shivered while her husband wrapped his arm around her and rubbed her shoulder.

Chip had disappeared into the office to talk to his fire chief, assuring him that everything was under control. He said the fire chief would've heard the 9-1-1 call through the radio and worried.

"We're just about done here," one of the paramedics announced to the group. He pulled off his latex gloves and balled them together. "The closest hospital is St. Vincent's, in case anyone wants to notify her next of kin."

Mary, Marty, and Robert looked to Samantha.

"Um…I know she co-owns a shop called Mystic Treasures on 4th and Walnut," Samantha said. "That's all I know, really."

Mary scoffed.

The man nodded. "That's where I'll start, then. Have a good night, everyone." He waved to the group and then stepped back out into the cold.

"What are we going to do?" Samantha asked once they were alone. She couldn't stop selfishly thinking about herself and her wedding since Talia first fell. And even though she was also worried about the woman who was supposed to marry them, Samantha mostly worried whether or not they'd even still be able to get married.

"We'll figure it out," Kathy said.

"How? The wedding is supposed to be in less than twenty-four hours!" Samantha's voice grew more shrill. "We have guests coming and flowers and catering, but no one to perform the ceremony."

"You could always get married in a church," Mary

murmured. "Even on short notice, I know Father Benson would—"

"That's not what we had planned," Samantha snapped.

"Well, your plans have obviously changed," Mary said. "The woman collapsed. It's not like she could control that. And maybe now is the perfect opportunity to get married in a—"

"Mom, that's not what we agreed on," Steven said. "Let's try to keep to the original plan as best we can."

Kathy reached for Samantha's hand. "Don't worry about finding another officiant. Let me take care of it."

"And how many officiants do you know?" Mary asked. "Unless, of course, you go to a church—"

"Mom!" Steven snapped.

"Actually, you'd be surprised who I can find." Kathy got to her feet and walked across the room toward the hallway with the bathrooms. "I'll be back once I've found someone!"

Samantha watched her sister walk off and then turned back around to bury her face in her hands.

"Honey, come on," Steven said. "Let's eat something and finish setting up. Kathy will take care of it. You'll feel better once you get something in your stomach."

She sat up and saw that Steven had pushed one of the sandwiches in front of her. The others sat around the table and began unwrapping the paper around their own subs.

"We had everything planned." She pushed away her food.

"This wasn't supposed to happen! We don't have enough money to cancel and reschedule everything last-minute! As much as I'm looking forward to tomorrow, I'm so *tired* of planning this wedding and navigating everyone's schedules!"

Perhaps you're not mature enough to get married.

The thought broke into Samantha's mind, which she heard distinctively in Mary's voice.

"Excuse me?" Samantha's eyes bore holes in her future mother-in-law.

Mary stared back, wide-eyed.

"You don't think I'm *mature*?" Samantha knew she had read Mary's mind with her power. The thought probably slipped through since Samantha was so stressed out and her control of that power was still relatively new.

Still, that line of thinking was something Samantha couldn't ignore. She resisted the urge to dig through more of Mary's mind to find out what she really thought of her, but that wouldn't help matters any.

Steven looked across the table between his mother and his future wife. "Nobody said any—" He stopped when it hit him what had happened.

"Well, dear, I just think that maybe you're being a bit insensitive," Mary said. "After all, this woman had a seizure. Surely, you can't get mad at her for that."

"I'm not mad at her, I'm frustrated with the situation," Samantha said. "And you're not helping any with all of your *subtle* suggestions. We chose Talia to perform the ceremony for a reason."

"A reason that hardly makes sense." Mary looked up and shook her head. "You didn't seem to really know the girl and she was…odd."

"What's wrong with odd? It's not like she was a bitch, unlike—"

"Sam!" Steven put his hand on her arm to stop her.

"No, dear, she was quite pleasant," Mary admitted. "Which makes it that much more curious to me why you can't drum up some compassion for a woman who's just been rushed to the hospital."

Samantha stared at her, completely lost for words, nearly shaking with anger.

"Mom, Talia's being taken care of," Steven said. "We called 9-1-1, they took care of it. What else do you expect us to do?"

"Perhaps go visit her or show a *little* remorse for her instead of being so consumed in your own affairs."

"We're getting married tomorrow," Steven started.

"Get out!" Samantha shouted.

Mary blinked and watched her curiously. "Excuse me?"

"You heard me." Samantha extended her hand to the door and pointed. "Get out of here. You've been making snide comments all evening and I'm tired of hearing it. If you're not going to help us figure out a solution, then you're only adding to the problem. So go."

Mary looked around the table. Marty and Robert were busying themselves eating up what was left of their subs. Robert kept his head low, trying to ignore the confrontation playing out across the table.

"Steven?" Mary asked quietly, her voice quivering.

"Right now you're really only causing more stress," he said in a somber voice.

Mary looked stricken and turned to her husband. The room had gone silent, with the only sound being Chip on the phone with the fire chief.

Marty looked to his son and then leaned over to Mary. "Why don't you just give them some space? Give everyone some time to calm down and the emotions to fade a bit."

With a huff, Mary rose and marched with her head held high to the hallway where Kathy escaped.

A moment later, Marty wiped his mouth with a napkin and murmured, "Excuse me," before rising and chasing after his wife.

CHAPTER 5

Kathy crouched on the toilet seat in the stall of the bathroom and tapped the end of the pen against her knee. She only had so much room to write on the small napkin she grabbed from the bag of subs on her way out. She didn't want to scribble every thought that came to her head like she usually did when she wrote spells.

Since they were looking for a magical officiant to perform the ceremony, Kathy wanted to cast a spell to call for a magical being. They didn't have time to search the old-fashioned way, like they did with Talia. That had just been dumb luck.

About a month ago, Kathy had been running some errands for Samantha for the wedding while she was at work. One of the stops on the list was Mystic Treasures for solomon's seal flowers and an assortment of the green tea light candles for the centerpieces. It was a little shop where they got most of their magical supplies.

They frequented it so much that the sisters suspected the shop's owners, Talia and Cassandra, were witches too, although there was never any confirmation offered. Kathy was assured by the fact that Talia and Cassandra couldn't run an occult shop without having a few secrets of their own.

When Kathy went there to get the stuff for the centerpieces, she had gotten to talking with Talia about how Samantha was getting married, but they still needed an officiant. Talia said that she was one and offered to perform the ceremony for free, since they were such loyal customers.

And now Talia was on the way to the hospital and here Kathy was sitting in a bathroom stall crafting a spell on a napkin to replace her.

None of this felt right to her.

Kathy scribbled out more notes on the napkin as she tried to write as quick as her thoughts, but gentle enough so as not to tear through the thin material. The pen slipped and she drew on her jeans a bit. Cussing under the breath, she licked her finger and tried to work off the spot before giving up and making a mental note to treat it when she got home.

Finally, when she felt she had gotten the spell right, she flipped the napkin over and wrote out the complete incantation on the back, which she'd intentionally left blank.

SORCERER

Standing, Kathy chewed on the end of the pen and considered if she should cast it now or wait until later. The image of her sister on the verge of hyperventilating because her wedding was about to fall apart came to Kathy and she made up her mind.

She would cast the spell now to help put Samantha at ease sooner. She wanted Samantha to fall asleep tonight excited about her wedding day tomorrow, not wondering if it'd even happen. Moving her hair out of her face, Kathy took a deep breath and began to recite the spell.

Magical spirits and powerful divinity,
I call you now to hear my plea.
We need someone to perform a ceremony.
Send someone here who can help me.

CHAPTER 6

Mary stepped into the hallway and turned out of sight of the group at the table before she sucked in the shuddering breath. Shortly after, Marty was beside her. He reached for her and pulled her into a hug, which she leaned into.

"Aw, honey," he cooed. "Don't let it bother you. It's just a lot going on right now."

Mary pulled away and whispered, "She's about to marry our son, Martin. Do you want to deal with this kind of turmoil every holiday or every time we have people over? I want to be able to see my son without having to walk on eggshells around *her*."

"I thought you two were getting along better?" he asked. "You've been helping with more things for the wedding and she invited you to get ready with her and her sister tomorrow."

"She's only including me because she needs my help."

He gave her a look. "That's not fair. Think of it from her side. She's trying to organize everything and now she needs to scramble to find an officiant at the last minute. It's a lot of stress and you *were* being a bit pushy."

"I wasn't making snide comments like she said I was. I was only offering suggestions."

"Whatever they were, they weren't helping," he said.

"But she's not even being reasonable."

"It's her wedding day. And that might not even happen if they can't find someone to marry them."

"But I suggested they move it to a church."

"And they've both already said they don't want it in a church," he said.

"But—"

"Honey, think back to our wedding day." Marty wiped a tear from his wife's face. "Imagine how disappointed you'd be if the bottom dropped out on us at the last minute. That's what Samantha's going through. I'm sure she just got caught up in the moment. I wouldn't be surprised if an apology comes sooner than later."

Mary nodded and reached for her husband again, who hugged her tight.

"Why don't you take five minutes, maybe get some fresh air or something, and then come back," he suggested. "But maybe keep your comments to yourself this time. If she asks you for advice, then offer your opinion, but only then." He smirked. "You have a habit of making your way seem like the *only* way."

She offered a weak smile in return. "Isn't that why you married me?"

Marty pulled her closed and kissed her cheek. "Cheer up. Our son is getting married tomorrow."

She watched him disappear around the corner before she turned and entered the bathroom.

Immediately, she heard Kathy's voice echoing in the small space. Words and rhymes. Mary was quiet as she listened, trying to determine what Kathy was saying.

Is there someone else in here? Did she bring a man into the bathroom with her? Chip was still on the phone and Robert was at the table. Everyone else is accounted for.

Mary took a step back and tried to peer under the stall for another set of feet, but she couldn't get the right angle in the small bathroom unless she bent over to look and she wasn't about to be labeled a Peeping Tom.

She started to move to the second stall, but stopped and caught a glimpse between the cracks of the stall walls. Kathy stood in front of the toilet, looking up toward the ceiling. Bright light flashed out from within and Mary realized Kathy had stopped speaking.

When she peeked through the crack again, she didn't see Kathy anymore, blocked instead by a larger figure in a heavy brown coat. Mary's eyes traveled up and she saw the top of his head peaking out over the top of the stall.

"Where am I?" The sound of the deep voice confirmed it wasn't Kathy speaking.

Mary's eyes went wide and her head spun. She didn't know what she had just witnessed. Her mind immediately went to the documentaries and news reports she had been seeing on the news about satanic rituals.

Did Kathy just summon a demon? Is Samantha involved too? Did she somehow get Steven roped into it too? Does he even know?

She took a deep breath to calm herself.

"We need your help," Kathy said.

"Who are you?" he asked.

"My name is Kathy. I'm a witch."

Mary gulped and she feared that Kathy or the man would discover her and kill her. Swinging open the bathroom door, she rushed back out into the hallway and started for the emergency exit, but turned back when she thought of Marty. If they came out of the bathroom and went on a killing spree for being found out, Marty would be a sitting duck. So would Steven.

Mary turned back to head into the rest of the fire hall, but stopped before she turned the corner. Looking back at the bathroom door, she noticed how Kathy and the mysterious man were still in there. If they had known Mary had walked in, they would've followed her out.

She forced herself to steady her breathing.

Maybe it's just Kathy who's a witch. Even Samantha has been so consumed with her wedding. Would witches care about that? Was it just a ruse to get Steven to be her husband? What would be the reason? What did Steven have to offer her, other than his love?

Mary shook her head to try to settle her thoughts. All she knew at this point was that Kathy was a witch. She'd have to be quiet and feel out Samantha and Steven.

If it turned out Samantha was a witch too, hopefully Mary could stop the wedding before it happened.

CHAPTER 7

Cassandra stood in front of the counter with her hands on her hips and looked around the shop. She had run out of things to do to keep her mind off the book. Not that she had been successful in that. Even as she straightened up the store, counted down the cash drawer, and added items to their inventory order, her thoughts remained on the mysterious book.

She brushed back the many bracelets on her arm to look at her watch. It was going on eight o'clock. Talia should've been home by now. She worried something had happened to her and damned herself for not having her write down the number for the wedding venue she was going to.

But they might have the number of the woman who hired her.

Cassandra moved behind the counter and pulled out a well-worn notebook that contained all of their customer orders. She wracked her brain trying to remember the name of the woman who had come in—the one Talia had talked about a wedding with.

She remembered they had ordered ragwort about two months ago and she flipped through the pages for the correct entry. Whenever they didn't have something in stock, she and Talia took special orders and called the customer when it came in, which required them to keep track of some customer names and phone numbers.

As she flipped through the book, she scanned each entry until she spotted the entry for ragwort. Holding her finger below the entry, she moved over to the name: Kathy Walker. Beside it a phone number was listed.

Cassandra picked up the phone and began to dial, but paused. What was she going to say?

"Can you send my girlfriend home? It's past her curfew."

"Can I talk to Talia? I'm afraid she's dead."

"Can you hurry your wedding planning along? I don't want to be alone."

Setting the phone back in the cradle, she pushed the customer order book aside and leaned on the counter, running her fingers through her short pixie-cut hair.

If it wasn't for that mysterious book showing up, Cassandra wouldn't be this paranoid. The fact that it had appeared completely unannounced was what was most terrifying to her.

Where had it come from? Someone must've sent it. But why here? And by whom?

Giving in, Cassandra turned and grabbed the book wrapped in the ritual cloth and set it on the counter in front of her. Carefully, she unwrapped it until it was sitting in the center of the cloth on the counter.

She pulled up a chair and examined the markings, being careful not to touch it directly. In the center of the book was an inverted pentagram, which had long been a symbol used to conjure evil spirits. That marking alone sent chills up her spine. She pulled her shawl a little tighter around herself, but the negative energy she felt from the book was enough to turn her blood cold. Still, she pressed on.

In the center of the pentagram was a symbol that Cassandra didn't immediately recognize. There was an arch over the top of a half circle with a swirl coming off the bottom and a narrow line jutting from the top. Just below the half circle was a diamond.

Even though she didn't know what it was, she knew where she could probably find it. She got up and crossed to the back of the shop and pulled out an encyclopedia of symbols. It was a doorstop of a book—one that Talia didn't think would ever sell—and Cassandra carried it back to the counter, pushing aside trinkets and pamphlets to make room for it.

Flipping through the pages, she opened the table of

contents to jump to the section she thought most appropriate. It took her a while to flip through all the symbols and their written entries, but eventually she found it: Luciferian eye, yet another demonic marking.

Sitting back, Cassandra considered opening the book to look for additional symbols to confirm what she already knew in her heart: this book was a grimoire, a magic book filled with dark magic that was meant to do harm, not good.

But the mystery remained: why was it here? How did it get here? Who had summoned it or sent it here?

Has Talia been dipping into dark magic? she wondered, but immediately put the thought out of her head. Talia wouldn't ever do that. Cassandra knew it in her soul.

The phone rang and Cassandra jumped. She clutched her chest to regain her composure and then reached beneath the counter to answer it.

"Mystic Treasures, this is Cassandra, how may I be of service today?" Absently, she covered the grimoire back up, deciding that she had had enough of it. She just wanted it out of her shop and as far away as possible.

"Hi, yes, this is Marie at Saint Vincent Hospital," a kind woman's voice said on the other end. "I'm trying to reach the next of kin for Talia Lawson. I was told she works at this shop."

Cassandra felt all of her breath suddenly rush out of her. "Did something happen to her?"

"I'm afraid I'm not at liberty to say—"

"I'm her partner," she said quickly. "I am her next of kin."

"Oh—oh, I see," the woman stammered. "Well, um…" She paused, then lowered her voice as if what she was about to say was a secret. "Miss Lawson was admitted to the hospital because she suffered a seizure. Now, the doctors say she's in a coma, although the cause is undetermined."

Cassandra's head was spinning. Talia didn't have any history with seizures and she was otherwise perfectly healthy.

"I'm on my way," she told the woman. Dropping the phone in the cradle, she snatched up her keys from the counter and bolted out the door.

CHAPTER 8

Steven shut the door to the utility room in the fire hall and turned to Samantha with crossed arms.

Samantha leaned against the large basin sink on the opposite side of the room. She knew why he had pulled her in here to talk privately. Blowing up at his mother like that was a line she had been so careful not to cross ever since they officially met.

"Look, I'm sorry about what I said to your mother," she started. "I'll apologize to her myself."

"You and I both know that's the right thing to do. And I'm sure she'll love to hear it." He stepped close to her and took her in his arms.

She leaned into his chest. "I'm just so stressed out about

what we're going to do."

"Kathy said she's working on it."

"But what if she doesn't find anyone? Then what are we going to do?" She groaned and pulled away from him to step toward the furnace in the corner. "Ugh, I know I sound like such a brat right now. I *do* feel bad about Talia. I wish it hadn't happened—for her sake and for ours. But it did and as much as I would love to go check up on her, I need to put out fires here first."

Steven came up behind her and rubbed her shoulders. "I know. Trust me, everyone here knows what you're going through. My mother, just needed some reminding." He chuckled.

She spun around and shot a look at him. "Steven, this isn't funny. We're supposed to be married by this time tomorrow. By the way it looks, that's not going to happen."

He took a step back, raised his eyebrows, and held a hand out toward her. "Okay, you need to calm down. You're getting a bit into the bridezilla mode again."

Samantha crossed her arms and took in a deep breath.

Steven spoke softly to her, proceeding with caution. "I know neither of us want to and it's going to cost extra to reschedule, but I think the best option here is to postpone the wedding until we find someone else who can marry us—or maybe Talia will recover and she can do it at another date."

She let out a heavy sigh and stared at the floor, making a

mental list of everyone she'd need to notify about the date change. It wouldn't be easy and it wouldn't be fun and she figured she'd be fending off rumors about her marriage being in trouble for the rest of her life from this postponement, but it was their only option.

"I don't *want* to move the date," she said. "But honestly, the choice isn't really ours anymore. This is what we have to do. Otherwise, we're just having a big party."

"Hey, parties are fun."

"Not when it was supposed to be a wedding." She tucked her hair behind her ears and rubbed her temples gently. "I just hope this isn't a sign."

"A sign of what?"

"Like, that it's not a bad omen or something. That you and I getting married is doomed from the start."

Steven pulled her in for another hug. "Sam, I'm not a witch and I'm not really that big into superstitions and all that—although you are bringing me around to the idea of fate. Regardless of all that, I know for a fact that we love each other. We have nothing to worry about."

For the first time since Talia collapsed, Samantha cracked a smile. She wrapped her arms around his neck and reached up to kiss him.

It was silly of her to think that this was the only chance she had to marry him. Even if she didn't marry him in the way she had planned, Steven was right: they loved each other. The fact of the matter was, they *would* get married. It just might be totally different than she expected.

When they parted, he held out his hand for her to take it. "What do you say? Do you think you're ready to make the announcement?"

She made a face. "I wish we didn't have to." Taking his hand, she stepped toward him. "But it's the right thing to do."

CHAPTER 9

"e need your help," Kathy told the figure squished in the bathroom stall with her.

"Who are you?" he asked. The most notable feature was his wide shoulders, made larger by the many layers he wore under his coat. He had a thick brown beard, speckled with gray hairs. A knit hat sat on his head, covering most of his forehead and resting just above his bushy eyebrows. In his hand he held a crooked wooden staff, like a thick walking stick.

"My name is Kathy," she said. "I'm a witch."

"What is a witch doing summoning me?"

"So you're magical?" she asked as a confirmation.

"Yes," he said. "I'm a sorcerer. Augustus."

Kathy wasn't too familiar with sorcerers, but he looked

ceremonial enough. Out of all the different evil forces she and Samantha had faced, none of them had been sorcerers. Not that that meant there weren't some bad eggs. Even witches could be bad sometimes. But at the moment, she was willing to take the risk for her sister.

"Well, Augustus, we're in a bit of a bind," she said. "See, my sister was supposed to get married tomorrow, but the woman she had scheduled to perform the ceremony had a, uh…medical emergency tonight. She'll be fine, but it's not likely that she'll be able to do the ceremony tomorrow."

Augustus stared at her with a blank expression. Kathy figured that was because she summoned him to a bathroom stall and started rambling about her sister. The poor guy was still in shock.

"Anyway," she went on. "I know this is kind of weird, with the circumstances and all, but I cast a spell to bring me someone who could perform ceremonies and you're the one who showed up. Do you think you could help us out?"

He narrowed his eyes and studied her.

"Just real quick tomorrow around two o'clock," she continued. "You can leave right after that if you want. My sister just wants someone magical to perform a magical ceremony that will bring hope and prosperity to her marriage without being *too* fire and brimstone, you know?"

Augustus took in the room, pressing his thick hands on the door to the stall. He didn't seem to even be listening to Kathy.

"So…what do you say?" she pushed.

He continued to study the room, turning to look for the door handle. "I don't do charity." He got the door open and stepped back, bumping into Kathy as he allowed the door to swing in.

She fell backward and reached for the wall to keep from falling into the toilet. She saw him step to the door to the hallway and stopped him.

"Wait! We're really kind of desperate here. If you do this for us, we'll owe you."

Augustus stopped and picked his head up. Slowly, he turned back to her.

Seeing that she caught his interest, Kathy elaborated a bit more. "We'll do anything—well, within reason, but pretty much anything, yeah. Whatever it is you need, we'll do it. Cast a spell of good fortune on your house? Done. Help you—I don't know—vanquish a dragon or something? Sure. We'll do it."

"And all I need to do is perform the wedding ceremony?" he asked.

"Yeah, that's it."

"The wedding is tomorrow?"

She nodded. "Yup. Right here. Well, over in the hall, not the bathroom. That'd be weird." She breathed in a deep breath to try to push away her nerves. "So what do you say?"

He turned to the door, then looked back at her. "Okay."

"Yeah?" She smiled wide. "Okay! Let's go tell everyone the good news!"

She stepped toward him to reach for the door and led him into the hallway. When she heard the murmur of voices around the corner, another thought came to her and she quickly turned to stop Augustus from going further.

"Just one more thing," she said. "Samantha and I are the only magical people here. Everyone else doesn't even know that it exists. So keep any mention of it—and any use of it—to an absolute minimum, if at all."

"I understand."

Kathy indicated his staff. "Perhaps you should set that aside while—"

"I would prefer to hold it," he said firmly.

"Okay then," she said with another breath. "Let's go tell everyone the good news."

CHAPTER 10

- DECEMBER 1988 -

Talia busied herself by watering the herbs lining the window. It was a relatively slow day, being after the winter solstice and, less importantly, Christmas. Mystic Treasures had already reached its monthly quota two weeks ago, thanks to the upsurge in orders for the solstice. They saw another little bump in sales in preparation for Christmas—many, *many* requests for authentic mistletoe.

Now that the two holidays were over, Talia and Cassandra could rest easy through the new year.

The bell over the door jingled and Talia turned to see another customer walk in. He was rather odd, which said a lot for the clientele the shop attracted. He wore a heavy fur coat and held an ornate walking stick. His face was bare, which, combined with his small frame, made him seem young.

"Can I help you?" Talia asked.

He turned and met her eyes. Any indication that he was just a boy faded by the intense look he gave her.

"Is—is there something in particular you're looking to find?" Talia tried to keep the fear from her voice. They'd had shoplifters—or worse, vandals—in the shop before and they'd handled their own, but this man was different.

In two long strides, he was standing right in front of her. Talia tried to step backwards, but bumped into a crate holding altar cloths. Regrettably, the phone—and the gun they kept for just these instances—was behind the counter on the other side of the room.

And Cassandra was upstairs meditating. Even if she heard Talia call out for her, the man would likely be gone—or worse—before Cassandra could make her way down to the shop.

"I'm looking for a book," he said in a gravelly voice.

She swallowed to try to moisten her throat. If she could get around him and scoot over to the counter, she would feel safer and maybe even be prepared to defend herself if it came to that.

"A book? What kind of book?"

Talia yelped when she felt something hard press against the front of her sweater, right above her stomach. She glanced down and saw the glint of a blade.

"It's a very *specific* book," he said. "Your magic book."

"I—I don't know what you're talking about," she lied.

The next moment, she felt the cold blade push through her sweater and press against her flesh.

"Don't lie, Talia Lawson," he said. "I know you're a witch. And I know you live with another witch, Cassandra Hoffman."

Talia gulped. "And who are you?"

The man sneered. "Ezra, sorcerer and heir to my family's grimoire, which I plan to add to from your magic book."

"You'll never—"

The bell above the door jingled again.

Talia locked eyes with the woman who stepped in. She'd been in the shop before to buy some herbs that she used to cook with, so she was fairly regular.

Ezra turned and watched the woman, who oblivious to the confrontation she interrupted. Slowly, he pulled the knife back into his fur coat.

"This isn't over," he told Talia. He stepped back, slipped by the new customer, and out to the sidewalk.

Talia quickly collected herself so her customer wouldn't notice how flustered she was. The last thing their business needed was for word to spread that it was a poor neighborhood rife with break-ins and threats. It already wasn't the best neighborhood, but it certainly wasn't the worst.

"Can I help you with something?" Talia asked. She tried to convey a friendly tone, but she could hear the tremor slip in.

"I'm just looking to get some herbs." The woman gave Talia a list of herbs and the amounts.

SORCERER

While Talia bagged up the dried herbs they stored behind the counter, she made a mental note to cast protection charms on the shop tonight and fill the space with incense. Sorcerers were nothing to tussle with and Talia didn't want another one lurking around anytime soon.

CHAPTER 11

When Mary rushed back into the fire hall, only Marty and Robert remained. They were stacking the extra chairs onto the carts to push back into the storage room. Despite the less-than-ideal location, even Mary had to admit that the fire hall looked nice.

But that wasn't what was foremost on her mind.

She ran straight to her husband and grabbed ahold of his arm with a tight grip.

"Easy, Mary, those fake nails of yours hurt." He shrugged her off and reached for another chair.

"Marty, we need to go."

He set the chair in line with the others on the cart. "Just a second. We're almost done."

Mary cast a look at Robert, who was on the other side of the room, no doubt trying not to eavesdrop. He was folding chairs and resting them against the wall instead of bringing them back to the cart beside Marty and Mary.

"I'm serious, let's go!" she pressed. "Something's not right here."

"What's your rush?" her husband asked.

Mary glanced over at Robert again before returning her gaze to Marty. She didn't want to get into the discussion right now about what she saw in the bathroom. She just needed to get them out of there. "I think I left the stove on."

Marty groaned. "Are you sure?" He lowered his voice. "This doesn't have anything to do with Samantha, does it?"

Mary swallowed hard and considered telling him no, but she didn't want to lie to him anymore than she had to at the moment. Besides, he would take it as her being mad at Samantha, when in reality she was just fearful of her and Kathy. "Let's just go," she said as her response. "I'll explain everything in the car."

Marty looked toward the utility room and said, "Steven and Samantha are talking about what they're going to do about tomorrow. We need to at least say goodbye."

Mary thought about their son and how close he was to Samantha and Kathy and everything they were involved with. Did he know their secrets? How could he not? Obviously, the sisters' mysteries didn't bother him—not enough to leave, which said enough about where he stood on the topic. Mary wondered where she went wrong as a mother.

"He's too involved already," she said. "Let's just go."

Marty furrowed his brow and stared at her. "What are you talking about?"

She stared into his eyes, seeing the worry, but the panic on her mind was completely driving her actions. "We need to go!"

"Not until you tell me what's going on!"

Behind Marty, Robert continued to pretend like he couldn't hear them.

Mary was about to blurt out what she saw in the bathroom—Robert be damned—but before she had the chance, the door from the utility closet opened and Steven and Samantha came out holding hands.

Marty put up a finger to his wife to tell her to wait, then stepped toward his son.

"Hey everyone," Steven said. "We've come to a decision."

Mary walked up and stood beside her husband. Her mind raced with ideas of how she could get both Marty and Steven out of the fire hall and to safety without raising alarm. She would even bring Robert, too, because he was completely innocent in all of this.

"Thank you all for coming out and helping us set up everything tonight," Samantha said, hanging on Steven's arm. "And for all of your help leading up to the wedding—especially you, Mary."

SORCERER

That took her by surprise and she clutched her chest. She was torn between being touched by the sentiment and concerned about the impending marriage.

"Unfortunately," Samantha went on, "due to today's unforeseen events, we think it'd be best to postpone the wedding until either Talia gets better or we find another officiant."

Mary rocked her head back and looked to the ceiling as relief washed over her. At least now she had some time to think of a way to stop the wedding from happening. Maybe even get the sisters arrested for whatever sinister things they were doing in that big creepy house.

And to think, I have had meals in that house! she thought.

"Wait a minute!" Kathy called out from around the corner near the bathrooms. "Don't announce anything yet!"

When she emerged into the hall, Mary recoiled toward her husband at the sight of the witch. She jumped again when she saw the burly man who had appeared in the bathroom follow Kathy out.

Mary's eyes darted over to Samantha and Steven to judge their reaction. Both of them seemed equally confused.

"Who is…?" Samantha started.

"I found another officiant," Kathy said with a big grin. "Everyone, this is Augustus."

Mary looked him up and down. After his size, the most notable thing about him was the large stick he held in his hand that stretched down to the floor. As if he were walking in the woods. Which made sense with everything else he was wearing—boots, hides, fur. He looked like he had walked right out of an Alaskan hike.

Of course, for all Mary knew, maybe he did. After all, Kathy had brought him to the hall from *somewhere*.

"Augustus?" Samantha asked skeptically.

Kathy nodded. "He's going to marry you guys."

The silence around the room was deafening as everyone stared at the large brute with the walking stick. Mary's eyes darted between the sisters and then her son. Steven seemed to be nervous about the newcomer, but he was the first to break the silence of the room and step forward with his hand out to greet Augustus.

"Hi, I'm Steven," he said. "The groom. Nice to meet you."

"This is ridiculous." Mary couldn't watch the exchange. She grabbed her coat and headed for the exit with her head shaking.

"Mom?" Steven's eyes followed her as she walked out.

"Mary!" Marty called after her.

She ignored them both and stepped out into the cold January night, which was the better alternative than staying inside with the circus her son was about to marry into.

Steven had completely lost his mind.

CHAPTER 12

Samantha walked into the house and flicked on the lights. Her shoulders were tense from the stressful car ride home. And yet, nobody said a word. She made Steven drive her own car with Augustus in the back seat while Kathy drove Steven's car home. Samantha didn't want Kathy alone with Augustus, and she wanted to keep an eye on Augustus in case he wasn't as trustworthy as Kathy believed.

The whole way home, Samantha tried to use her power to fish through Augustus's mind, but she couldn't get anything. She didn't know if that was because she still had to get a handle on her newest power or if Augustus was blocking her attempts somehow. She tried not to think about it.

Shortly after she walked into the house, Steven and

Augustus followed. Kathy was still on her way.

"Did you want to hang up your coat?" Samantha pointed to the coatrack behind the door.

Augustus glanced at it, but ignored her comment. He stepped into the house and looked around the various rooms, still dark from the evening. Samantha hadn't been home since she left for work in the morning and she was looking forward to the time off she had scheduled for the next week.

"So, Augustus," Steven started, "why don't you tell us a little more about yourself?"

The man turned and looked at him. "Why?"

"Well, I just thought that since you'll be marrying us, we shouldn't be strangers," Steven said.

"Where did my sister find you?" Samantha asked.

"Magic," he said.

She nodded and ran her tongue over her teeth. "Perfect. Yup. That's great."

Suddenly, Kathy walked in and shut the door behind her. "Burr! It's so cold out there!" She pulled off her scarf and hung it on the coat rack, then slipped out of her black pea coat and hung that as well. She passed off the car keys to Steven. "Your chariot awaits, mister!"

"Thanks," he said.

Augustus peered through the dark rooms before returning to the foyer and studying the ceiling, outlined by oak trim and plaster details around the small chandelier.

"So." Kathy looked between them all. "What have you guys been talking about?"

"Just trying to get to know each other a bit better," Steven said.

"Oh, that's nice!" She turned to the man. "Do you prefer Augustus or can we call you August or Auggie or Gus Gus or something?"

"Gus Gus?" Samantha asked.

Kathy shrugged.

The man shook his head. "My name is Augustus."

"Kathy? A word?" Samantha turned and walked toward the kitchen, rubbing her neck. She turned on the light and stepped to the stove, where she set a kettle on a burner for some chamomile tea. She knew she was going to have trouble sleeping.

"It's pretty great that Augustus was able to save the day, huh?" Kathy said with a forced smile.

"Did you cast a spell to summon him?"

"Why do you ask that?"

"Because he told me you found him with magic."

"Well…I—"

"Kathy! We have enough trouble popping up around here as it is, we don't need you *summoning* anymore of it!"

"But Augustus isn't trouble," Kathy countered. "He's going to help us—help *you*. Besides, where was I supposed to find another officiant on such short notice?"

"Oh, I don't know. The *yellow pages*?" Samantha tucked her hair behind her ears and crossed her arms. "Okay, you understand my hesitation to this, right? I mean, we haven't had any magical problems since the shapeshifter across the street. We've been on a good streak! I thought maybe we could make it through my wedding day without any problems. And now you're telling me that you invited strange men into our lives the night before the wedding?"

Kathy wagged her finger. "Um, no. Not *men*, one man. And I only did it because I was trying to *save* your wedding. Augustus is harmless."

"You don't know anything about him."

"True, but I worded the spell very carefully. He's only here to help us. He's just…a little out of touch with the twentieth century."

"A little? Kathy, he's carrying a cane!"

"It's a staff," she corrected. "It must mean something to him."

Samantha scoffed. "Like that makes it better."

"Don't act like Talia was the perfect image of normalcy either! She was just as strange, but she was a woman so you're not judging her as hard."

"Well, to be fair, Talia doesn't look like she could strangle us with her bare hands," Samantha said.

"But that doesn't mean her magic couldn't."

The kettle whistled and Samantha turned to pull it off the burner.

"Look, after tomorrow at two, Augustus will be gone and you and Steven will be married," Kathy said. "Consider this my gift to you two."

Samantha looked over her shoulder and cocked an eyebrow. "The night before the wedding and you *still* didn't get us anything?"

Kathy shrugged. "It was on my to-do list, which has been pretty long, if I do say so myself. Being a maid of honor is no joke—and it's certainly not cheap."

Samantha dipped the tea bag in the water in her mug and started to head back to the foyer. "All I'm saying is, please don't let there be anymore surprises, okay? I'm already stressed out enough as it is."

Kathy followed behind her. "Yes, ma'am."

Back in the front of the house, Steven rested against the doorframe into the living room while Augustus flipped through the few books they had on a bookshelf behind the couch. His staff rested gently against his chest and a pile of discarded books lay on the seat of the couch.

"Just doing some light reading?" Samantha asked.

"He said he's looking for a particular book," Steven said.

"We have some more in the upstairs hallway," Kathy offered. "And in the spare bedroom."

"Spare bedroom?" Steven looked between Samantha and Kathy. "He's not staying here, is he?"

Samantha motioned toward him with her mug. "Well, we're

not exactly going to set him up at a Days Inn, now are we?"

Steven stood and put his arm around Samantha, leading her away from the living room. "I'm not sure I feel comfortable with him staying here alone with you guys. You barely know him."

"Well, if he's good enough to marry us, I think he's good enough to sleep in an old twin bed in the coldest room in the house," Samantha said.

"But it'll be just the two of you," he said. "I'm going back to my apartment to stay there."

Samantha gave him a patronizing smile and patted his arm. "I love it that you want to protect me, sweetie, but no offense, Kathy and I would handle ourselves better in this situation than you would."

"Hey." Steven stood up a little straighter and pulled at the lapels of his jacket. "I handled my own with the shifter."

"Yes, and what happened across the street a few months ago is exactly why I want you to stay as far away from any dangers as possible," Samantha said. "Besides, Kathy doesn't seem to think Augustus is anything to worry about. I'm leaning toward trusting her gut on this one."

"And what about *your* gut?" he asked. "What's that telling you?"

"It's telling me that I need to worry about the wedding and that by this time tomorrow, we'll only have to worry about something *much* more fun—like our honeymoon." She kissed him and smiled.

"Well, I better get home so tomorrow can come faster then." He kissed her again. As he turned to head to the door, he stopped to look at Augustus again.

"Are you hungry?" Kathy asked the man. "Or do you want anything to drink? Maybe you want to take a shower or something?"

"You can bring me food in the morning," Augustus told her.

Steven turned back to Samantha and muttered, "Are you sure you're going to be okay?"

"Yes," Samantha told him in a soft voice, even though she was asking herself the same question. "Look, I'll call you if anything goes bump in the night. But Kathy and I have handled much worse. Augustus may be a brute—and he's certainly odd—but he's no match for two witches."

Steven smiled and leaned down to kiss her again. "Okay then. I guess the next time I'll see you will be when you're walking down the aisle."

Samantha felt her body flush warmly with the thought. She couldn't believe that after all of the planning and struggling, they were finally about to get married. She could hardly wait much longer.

"I love you and I'll see you tomorrow," she told him.

"Love you too," he said as he started to the door. "Be safe!"

CHAPTER 13

Cassandra rushed into the hospital room and saw Talia laying in the bed, motionless, buried under a series of cords and wires hooked up to various parts of her body. Tears immediately filled Cassandra's eyes and she pulled up a chair close to the bed and took Talia's hand.

"Oh, baby, what happened?"

The only response was the consistent chirp from the monitor measuring Talia's heartbeat.

Cassandra couldn't help but wonder if Talia somehow got mixed up with whoever sent that book to their shop. Maybe Talia was supposed to receive it and not Cassandra? But then why was Talia the one in the hospital?

A blonde woman wearing purple scrubs with a stethoscope

around her neck walked in. She held a clipboard in her hand and went right to work checking Talia's charts. Cassandra pulled her hand away from Talia's and wiped her eyes. The nurse offered a polite smile as she checked the monitors Talia's wires were hooked up to.

"What's going on with her?" Cassandra asked. "Why isn't she waking up? Is that normal for people who have seizures?"

The nurse gave her another tight-lipped smile. "Not unless they've hit their head, no."

"So then why isn't she waking up?" Cassandra wiped the tears away with the edge of her sleeve and sniffled. "I'm assuming a doctor's looked at her. What's the diagnosis? What's the plan moving forward? How long will it be before she's back to normal?"

The nurse hugged the clipboard against her chest. "I'm sorry. But I can only disclose that kind of information with family."

"Talia doesn't have any family...not anymore." One of the hazards of their love was isolation. She tried to swallow the lump in her throat. "I'm her partner."

The nurse's eyes widened and she nodded slowly. "Oh. Oh, I see." She looked out into the hallway, then back to Cassandra. She went over and closed the door until there was only a small crack left opened. Then she stepped closer to Cassandra.

"Talia experienced a seizure," she started. "Luckily, she wasn't alone at the time and first responders got to her right away. But still…she hasn't woken up, as most people do after they've had an event like that."

"What does that mean?" Cassandra felt more tears pooling her eyes. She worried that Talia was a vegetable. Breathing, but not processing much else. No longer capable of the endless philosophical chats the two of them shared, or the vast knowledge of herbal care, or even basic human functions like walking and eating. The biggest fear Cassandra had was the unknown of what their future would look like.

The nurse took a deep breath. "We're not sure what it means yet. So far, the tests we have run show that she's very much alert. There doesn't seem to be any trauma to her brain. We still have some more tests to run to rule out any other issues, but for the time being, it looks like Talia will wake up when she's ready to. We're watching her closely. We're not going to let anything happen to her."

Cassandra nodded and looked to Talia, feeling relieved. "Good. Thank you. I appreciate it. I know you didn't have to tell me—a lot of people wouldn't."

"There's no reason to make this even more difficult for you," she said. "But I do have some questions, since you're here."

She braced herself for the invasive questions about their lifestyle. Half of the ones who didn't write them off as the scum of society really just wanted to know personal details they wouldn't ever dare ask any other couple.

"Does Talia have any history with epilepsy?" the nurse asked.

Cassandra's eyes widened. It wasn't what she expected to hear—although she should have. "Um…no. Not that I know of."

"No one in her family does?"

"Um…I don't know." Cassandra had only briefly met Talia's family. Back when she was still just her "friend." And since they had cut her off, Talia had done the same to them, not even mentioning her family at all.

The nurse looked at Talia and then down at her chart. "Hmm…I was hoping that might help explain why she's not waking up, but I guess we'll have to find another reason." She pulled her ID tag over the clipboard and showed it to Cassandra. "My name is Dawn. If you have any other questions or are having any problems getting in to see Talia, have them page me."

Cassandra felt like she could cry from the act of kindness alone. "Thank you so much! I truly do appreciate it."

The nurse gave her a warm smile. "Take care. I hope Talia wakes up soon."

When Cassandra and Talia were alone again, she took a seat beside the bed and took Talia's hand in hers.

"Don't worry," she told her because now she knew that Talia was listening. "I'm going to figure out what happened and fix it. This is definitely magical."

CHAPTER 14

Steven wandered into the living area of his apartment with his toothbrush hanging out of his mouth. He looked around at the organized mess. Boxes were everywhere. Some were stacked in the corner, fully packed and ready to move. Others sat in various places throughout the apartment waiting to be filled: the dishes from the kitchen, towels from the bathroom, and all of his work clothes hanging in the closet in his bedroom.

He was going to miss this place, even if it had caused him slight embarrassment from the moment he moved in. The apartment certainly wasn't the most elegant place he'd ever lived, but it was his. His first home, independent of his parents. But now that chapter of his life was coming to a close and he looked forward to the next one: being Samantha's husband.

Of course, he was still determined to convince Samantha to get their own place separate from Kathy, but among all of the other decisions to make about the wedding, he'd let that argument slide.

Steven returned to the bathroom and spit in the sink, then rinsed his brush before returning it to the cup on the tiny vanity. He turned on the hot water and waited for it to warm up before he washed his face. With his finger dipped into the running water, he heard the phone ringing and turned off the faucet to answer it.

Tossing the towel over his shoulder, he picked up the phone from where it sat in the corner of the kitchen counter. "Hello?"

"Steven, it's your mother," she said in a tone that he knew meant she was on edge. "Are you alone?"

"Yes." Better to keep his answers short and precise for both of their benefit. Steven's fuse with her was shorter when she got like this.

"Good, good," she said with a breath. "I need to talk to you about something serious and I want you to really think this through before you write it off."

Steven's mind raced with the possibilities of what she could want. Inviting people to the wedding at the last minute—people she had probably already told to come before checking with him. Changing the arrangement of the flowers that were going to be delivered tomorrow. Or possibly even changing the venue to a church—she hadn't ever really given up on that.

"What is it?" he asked, trying to keep the annoyance out of his voice.

"You need to call off the wedding."

"Ha!" The sound erupted from Steven before he could even think about keeping it in. He shook his head and smiled. His mother was really something.

"You promised you were going to give it some thought."

"No, Mom, *you* said I should give it some thought," he corrected. "This is insane. The wedding is *tomorrow*."

"I know, but what happened tonight—"

"Are you talking about Samantha's outburst after Talia went to the hospital? We talked about that. She was just stressed out from having to find an officiant, but Kathy took care of it."

"That's exactly it! Where did that man come from?"

"Augustus? I don't know," he lied. "Look, Mom, he's certainly a little strange, but that's okay." He noted the irony of how not even an hour ago, he was worrying about Augustus staying with the girls overnight and here he was telling his mother that the newcomer was perfectly tame. "He seems fine."

"He looks like he just spent a week sleeping on the ground!"

"The walking stick? Yeah, that's kind of weird, but it doesn't make him a rabid animal or anything. It's just a quirk. We all have them."

"I think this goes way beyond personality quirks," she pushed. "Steven, where did that man come from? Kathy didn't take her coat with her, so she probably never even left the building, yet she found an officiant within twenty minutes? It doesn't add up to me."

Steven suspected his mother had more to say than she was letting on, but he let her talk. Eventually it would all come out. She wasn't one to leave anything unsaid.

"And then the man she found," she continued. "Ugh, he's a piece of work, isn't he? So strange. And he didn't seem to know Kathy whatsoever, but they were pushing him on us like it was all normal."

"Samantha and I don't want to postpone the wedding."

"But you said you would earlier!"

"That's because we thought it was our only choice," he countered. "Before Kathy found Augustus."

His mother groaned on the other end. "I don't know. I don't trust those girls."

"Oh, so now it's Kathy too?"

"Well, she—"

"If you didn't notice—and I'm sure you didn't—Samantha thought the whole wedding was falling apart, less than twenty-four hours before it was supposed to happen," Steven said. "And since Kathy loves her, she was determined to find someone to replace Talia to keep the show on the road. *That's* how family supports each other. Not trying to cancel one of the most important days in a person's life the day before it happens."

"Honey, that's not what I'm doing." Her voice was more

desperate now. "Of course I want to see you happy. I just don't think this is it."

Steven sighed and rolled his eyes.

"When I went to the bathroom, I saw Kathy—"

"Well, lucky for you, Kathy isn't the sister I'm marrying." Steven's patience had grown thin. It was time to put his foot down. He couldn't believe his mother was still playing this game so close to the wedding.

"No, but honey—"

"Whatever concerns you have with Kathy, you can bring up with her directly," he went on. "After tomorrow, you and Kathy probably won't see much of each other anyway."

"Steven, listen to me! They're not good people! They're—"

"Good night, Mother," he said abruptly. "I need to get some sleep before I marry the woman I love tomorrow. If you call me anymore about this I'm going to unplug the phone."

"Steven—"

He set the phone down in the cradle, took a deep breath to calm himself—something he had picked up from Samantha recently—and returned to the bathroom to finish getting ready for bed.

Hopefully he wouldn't have any trouble falling asleep.

CHAPTER 15

S teven! Steven, listen to me!" Mary pulled the phone away and looked at it. "He hung up on me!"

She turned to her husband, who lay back on the couch with his neck twisted at an odd angle. Loud snores erupted from his open mouth with each passing breath.

"Marty!" She swatted his arm. "Marty, wake up!"

He jolted awake at the second slap. "Huh? What's the matter?" He licked his lips and clapped his mouth open and closed a few times to moisten it again.

"I just called Steven and he won't even *listen* to me about canceling the wedding," she said. "And he hung up on me!"

"I'm sure it was an accident." Marty leaned forward on his knees and looked around. The TV played quietly in front of them, but neither of them were paying too close attention.

"He told me if I called back, he was going to disconnect the phone," she said. "I think Samantha's gotten to him with whatever voodoo she's into."

Marty gave her a sideways glance. "Are you sure you saw what you saw in the bathroom at the hall?"

Mary had given him the run-down on the way home—filled with all of her conspiracy theories. Marty had sat and listened patiently, without saying much. Mary knew that what she saw was illogical, but she saw it with her own two eyes. She couldn't deny it, no matter how unbelievable it seemed.

And yet it explained so much about why the sisters were so strange. Not in the outwardly way that Talia—or certainly Augustus—were, but in more subtle ways. Like the mysterious disappearance of their father and the rest of their family, why Kathy couldn't hold down a job—or a man—and that creepy old house they lived in.

Whatever those sisters were into, Mary was determined to get to the bottom of it and make Steven see some sense again. She hoped she wasn't too late.

"Of course I saw it!" Mary said. "First, I heard Kathy chanting, then a flash of light, and suddenly that man—Augustus—was in the stall with her. The same one who is supposed to marry my baby to that devil woman." She leaned over and drove her finger into the couch cushion to further make her point. "*This* is exactly the reason I wanted them to get married in a church. It's probably why Samantha doesn't want to—her skin would erupt in flames if she ever stepped foot in a holy place."

"Is that what you saw or are you filling in the blanks with your imagination?"

"I *saw* it, Martin! I'm not crazy! I'm trying to protect our son. It doesn't seem like you care that much."

Marty took a deep breath. "Of course I care. I just think we're going to make ourselves the enemy by coming on this strong."

"So I'm supposed to roll over and let this happen? Let our son get sucked into the trenches of this girl's delusions?"

"I just think we need more information," Marty said.

"We don't have time for that! The wedding is in a little more than *twelve hours*!"

Marty sighed again. "So what do you want to do about it then?"

She looked toward the TV. Calling Steven had been a bust and calling Samantha probably wouldn't be much better. Certainly, she wouldn't admit to anything Mary would accuse her of. There would be no honest answers exchanged. Only misleading lies. The same way she probably roped Steven into her grip.

Marty gave up waiting for an answer from her. He rose to his feet and murmured, "Just think it through before you do anything crazy." She watched as he walked off toward their bedroom.

Mary returned her attention back to the TV and saw a new program starting. One of those late-night "news" stories that were a little out-there, but still within the grasp of reality. Flashed at the bottom of the screen were the words, "Is there a Satanic cult in your neighborhood?"

Frantically, she reached for the remote control to turn up the volume.

"…trend across the country where good, happy, and successful people are turning to dangerous groups that exhibit cult-like behavior to do something so out-of-the-ordinary, they need to do it in hiding: worship the devil."

Mary brought a hand to her mouth and watched with horror as her mind raced with the connections to Steven. He was a good, hardworking man, and now he's giving up his apartment to live with the sisters—further indoctrinating himself into their world. Worse, he was marrying her—did he really love her or was it just a cover for their Satanic worship?

When the narrator on the TV spoke of animal sacrifices to perform these odd rituals, Mary shot to her feet. Marty was right. She needed to do something about this.

Rushing over to the phone book by the phone, Mary began searching for the number to the local news channel. She knew nobody would answer so late, but she could leave a tip for someone to respond to in the morning. She needed to do something drastic before Steven was too far gone. There was no evidence for her to go to the police with—and she knew

SORCERER

Samantha, Kathy, and even Steven wouldn't ever crack. Maybe having the news in their face would get one of them to admit to something. If nothing else, it might delay the wedding.

When she found the number, she reached for the phone with a shaky hand and her fingers hovered over the dial pad while her eyes flicked up to the TV again. On the screen, several groups of people dressed in dark clothing and black make-up, marched through a cemetery wielding pentagrams and other occult symbols.

Feeling as if the air had been knocked out of her, Mary dialed the number for the station and pressed the phone to her ear, listening to it ring.

CHAPTER 16

Augustus opened the door from the spare bedroom and peered into the hall. It was late. The witches had gone to bed hours ago. If there was any perfect time to search the house for their magic book, it was now. He had already searched the spare room and didn't find anything.

He knew there was a magic book somewhere in the house. Most witches had them. He'd stolen them from witches before, transferred the knowledge into his own family grimoire, and then destroyed the books to never be used by that witch's family again. He intended to do the same with these witches' magic book, but first he would need to find it—and his family's grimoire. Until he found what was rightfully his, the witches' magic book could serve as a substitute.

Sorcerer

Stepping into the hall with his staff in hand, Augustus cringed when the floorboards beneath him creaked. Watching the two closed bedroom doors in the hall, he stepped further, ignoring additional creaks, and descended the staircase down to the first level. He had tried searching some of the bookshelves earlier when he first arrived at the house, but he knew they wouldn't be hiding it in plain sight. Witches liked to keep their magic a secret.

Instead, Augustus shifted his attention to more unlikely hiding spots: in the fireplace flue, under the furniture, in the built-in bench by the front door. The more he looked, the more frustrated he got from not finding it.

Worse, he realized how much he actually needed it. Ezra had hidden the grimoire very well. So well that none of Augustus' spell castings had resulted in any concrete lead. He thought that once Ezra was dead, the spells he had cast would be weakened—or removed—but apparently he had found another way to hide the book, even beyond his death.

Frustrated, Augustus threw his fists into the cushion of the couch, but it wasn't nearly rewarding enough. He wanted to flip the couch over. Toss it out the window. Do *something* to cause damage.

But that would alert the witches. Give away his secret, which they had been very oblivious about—too consumed in their own personal lives to understand what they had invited into their home. And yet he needed to keep them occupied in their activities until he found their book and could use it to help locate *his* book.

Then he could kill them.

Augustus stepped toward the kitchen, staff in hand, to search through the rest of the house for more hiding places, but he stopped as he passed the staircase. Someone upstairs was moving. If either of the witches noticed he was no longer in his room, his cover would be blown and then he would have no hope of finding their book—depending on how well they'd hidden it.

He started up the stairs, again cringing with each creak and groan of the old woodwork beneath his feet. By time he reached the top, he saw that the closest bedroom door was open. Augustus took a big step forward toward his own room, but stopped when the door on the other side of the hallway swung open.

"Oh!" Samantha pressed a hand to her chest and took half a step back into the bathroom. She wore a long-sleeve black shirt and plaid pajama bottoms with fuzzy socks. "You scared me." She pulled the sleeves of her shirt over her fists and crossed her arms in an effort to keep warm.

Augustus nodded curtly at her and stepped toward the spare bedroom.

"Is everything all right?"

He turned back to her. "Everything is fine."

Samantha looked down the stairs. "Then what were you

doing down there?"

"I was looking for another bathroom," he said.

She stepped across toward her bedroom and then pointed to the room she had just come out of. "The bathroom is right here."

Augustus nodded again and gave her what he thought was a disarming smile, but the witch continued to study him, even as he stepped toward the bathroom. "Good night."

She retreated further into her room, but waited for him to close himself in the bathroom before he heard her shut her bedroom door.

Inside, Augustus looked at himself in the mirror and wondered if he'd just blown his cover. He would have to wake up early to search the house for the book before the witches got up. He might not have much more time than that.

CHAPTER 17

- DECEMBER 1988 -

Ezra sat at the Hickory Nut Inn on the edge of the Allegheny Forest, enjoying his beer at the bar. It was a very modest place. Small, built from cinderblocks that were painted a bright green. A jukebox sat in the corner, playing classic rock. Several other gruff patrons sat down the bar, watching the news or sports on the two TVs above the liquor display.

The stool next to him squeaked as someone took a seat. Ezra looked up and saw none other than his brother, Augustus. He nodded a hello.

Augustus held up a finger to the bartender to order his own beer, then turned to Ezra. "You have an heirloom that belongs to me."

Ezra calmly sipped his beer. "That heirloom equally belongs

to both of us, brother."

"Exactly, and you've had it long enough."

"I need it."

"So do I."

"You'll abuse it."

"And you're not?"

"I'm still using it."

"So you have it here with you?"

"I didn't say that."

The bartender set Augustus's beer in front of him and then returned to cleaning glasses at the sink under the bar.

"Where is it?" Augustus asked, leaving his beer where it sat. "I'll track it down if I have to."

"Good luck trying to find it." Ezra thought back to that witch in Erie he had approached earlier that day. He knew his brother would come looking for him sooner or later. Knew it was only a matter of time before he'd have to hide the grimoire to make sure it didn't fall into Augustus's hands.

Ezra's trip to that witch in Erie was a way to test what his magic had already shown him: the woman was a witch and would recognize the grimoire for what it was. If he hid the grimoire with her, there were two options that might happen, both of which were manageable.

Option One: She would recognize the grimoire for what it was and hide it for fear of it spreading its dark magic. Whatever way the witch hid the grimoire—magically or physically—Ezra was confident that his powers would be able to trump hers and he'd easily locate it once he got Augustus off his back.

Option Two: The witch would touch the grimoire and maintain its secrecy so she could harness its power herself. Again, Ezra knew that a witch's magic paled in comparison to his own. He'd be able to overpower her in that instance—possibly even kill her and take her powers—and he'd have the book back to himself.

"What about a contract," Augustus said. "I'll take the…*heirloom* for a week. I'll bring it back to you next week, right here."

Ezra let out a loud, "HA!"

His response only enraged Augustus. Slamming his fist on the bar, the other sorcerer shot to his feet and bellowed, "You can't keep it from me for long, Ezra!"

"Hey!" the bartender shouted. "If you two are going to fight, take it outside! I'm not dealing with that shit in here!"

Augustus started to the door, then turned when Ezra remained in his seat. "Let's handle this outside like men, brother."

Ezra took a final sip of his beer and lifted it to indicate he wanted another. "I'm enjoying my drink right now, Augustus. We'll have to take up the childish fighting some other time."

"You're not going to face me like a man?"

"I don't need to," Ezra said.

"You were the one who's starting shit," the bartender added. "Get out of here! Don't let me see you in here again."

Ezra kept his back to his brother, but knew he was eyeing him up. After a minute, the door slammed as Augustus left.

The bartender gave Ezra a fresh bottle, then tossed his bar rag on the counter. "You mind keeping an eye on the place? I've had a few break-ins lately and I don't want this disgruntled jerk to be another. I want to make sure that guy makes it back to his car."

Ezra nodded. "You got it, man."

After the bartender left, Ezra took a look at the guys at the other end of the bar. They were so enraptured by the TVs that they weren't paying any attention to anyone else around them.

Opening his fur coat, Ezra pulled out the grimoire and the knife he had used on the witch in Erie. The tip of the blade still had a smidgen of her blood on it, which would be necessary to cast his spell.

Setting the knife on top of the book, Ezra grabbed his staff and gently tapped it on the floor to summon his power. He muttered a foreign spell and tapped his staff against the floor again.

In a blink of an eye, the grimoire disappeared from the bar top, sent to appear at the witch's shop in the event of his death. In the meantime, it was in the ether. Still within his grasp, but nowhere on earth for Augustus to track.

The bartender came back in just as Ezra was pocketing the bloodied knife.

"All set?" he asked.

"Yeah, that fool's long gone."

CHAPTER 18

Mary clutched her cup of coffee in her hands and stared at the table in front of her. Her eyes were unmoving, as was the rest of her. All except her mind, which hadn't stopped racing with a million what-if scenarios.

Through the windows at the front of the house, the sun had just begun to shine through. It looked like it was going to be a beautiful day. It had even snowed some last night to give everything a nice fresh coat of snow to cover up the dirty and half-melted mounds.

"You're up early," Marty said as he emerged from the bedroom.

Slowly, Mary's eyes flicked up to him. "Huh?"

He came up behind her, kissed her on the top of the head,

and hugged her from behind. "Cheer up. Our son is getting married today."

She groaned and shrugged him off of her.

He walked behind the kitchen island and fixed himself a cup of coffee. "I take it a good night's sleep didn't help you feel any better about it."

"I didn't sleep," she said. "Couldn't. This isn't good, Mart. I just can't shake the feeling that this wedding is a bad idea."

"Well, you've said your piece. Other than calling Steven up this morning and trying again, I don't know what else you could do." He took a sip, then added, "If you ask me, I think you should try to get some shut-eye before we get rolling with the wedding stuff. I'm sure it'll help you feel better. How much time do you have before you go over to the girls' house to get ready?"

"I'm not going," she said firmly.

Marty paused. She could hear him taking deep breaths, as if he needed to prepare himself for what would be a long conversation. He had been doing it their whole marriage as a way to calm himself down from the sometimes difficult discussions with her.

She knew she was a handful at times, but this was different. She wasn't going to let Steven marry someone she didn't trust. They had raised him to take care of himself, but everyone made mistakes. How could she be sure that he wasn't about to make a mistake now?

"Are you at least going to call them to let them know?"

Marty finally asked.

"No."

Another sigh. "Mary, come on. I know you're having a hard time with this, but you need to at least try to play nice with the woman who is about to be family."

"She will never be—"

The phone ringing cut her off. Since Marty was closest to it, he answered it.

"Hello?"

Mary watched nervously as she listened in on one side of the conversation. On a day like this, it could be anybody. Maybe it was Steven calling to say he thought about what she said and he was going to cancel the wedding after all.

"From where?" Marty asked. He looked over at his wife with his eyebrows scrunched together.

No, couldn't be Steven. Not with that expression on his face.

"Oh—okay," he murmured. "Just a sec. Here she is." He covered the receiver and held it up for Mary. "It's for you. Someone from the TV station. WICU, I think he said."

For the first time all morning, she jumped up with excitement.

"Did you call them?" Marty asked her.

She ignored him and took the phone from him. "This is Mary Harper."

"Hi Mrs. Harper, this is Eddie Richers. I'm a news reporter at WICU-TV. I got your message about your daughter-in-law—"

"No, she's *not* my daughter-in-law," Mary corrected. "My son just thinks he's going to marry her. They're *supposed* to get married today, but I'm not going to let that happen. There is definitely something going on with those girls—"

"Girls?" Eddie asked. "He's marrying two girls?"

"No, no. He's only involved with one of them, but she has a sister who I saw conjure a man out of thin air last night! And then she says he's going to marry them today! I tell you, this man they got is quite strange. He's a real wacko. I mean, the first woman they got to officiate the wedding was strange too—I think she might have an *alternative* lifestyle, if you know what I mean. Sadly, she had a seizure last night, which is also rather puzzling since I'm not one to believe in coincidences. I wonder if she did something that made the girls mad and they cursed her—"

"Ma'am, this sounds like an exaggerated story," Eddie cut in. "Are you sure this wasn't a dream or something?"

"I'm not making this up!" she shouted. "The girl they originally got to officiate the wedding, her name is Talia. She owns a weirdo shop somewhere in the city. She just had a seizure last night and was taken to Saint Vincent's—look into that. I'm not lying about that. And then—*poof!*—within twenty minutes they have a new officiant. Someone nobody has ever met before, who doesn't seem to be from around here. And I *saw* them pull him out of thin air! I promise you!"

Eddie paused for a moment. "Right. Well, I'm not sure this

is even a story I'd be able to tell with our medium. Unless someone's willing to go on camera—"

"I'll go on camera. I can show you where the one sister cast a spell or something."

"A spell?"

"She snuck into the bathroom—probably thought she was alone—chanted some words, and then a burst of light came and suddenly there was a man in there with her. I *saw* it!"

Eddie sighed and Mary worried she was losing his interest.

"Look, check into Talia and her freak shop," Mary told him. "Call the hospital and verify that she was taken there because of a seizure. And especially look into these girls: Samantha and Kathy Walker. My son is about to marry Samantha *today*. Look into them and then give me a call. But do it quick! We don't have a lot of time."

"Ma'am, we're not in the business to settle family disagreements," he said. "We're here to report the news."

"This is news! You should *want* to warn people about Satan worshipers who live in Erie! They're going to bring chaos to this entire city! Just look what they did to that poor girl last night!"

"Wait, wait—*Satan* worshipers?"

"Yes!"

"Have you seen any cult-like paraphernalia?"

"Um…" Mary thought about the many times she'd been in their house as they planned the wedding. "They have a lot of herbs growing. And candles. And old books. And their house! It's so creepy!"

"I need a little more than 'creepy' to go off of, ma'am."

"I've given you plenty," Mary persisted. "Look, check into those people—did you write down their names? Once you look into them, meet me at their house. I'm supposed to go there this morning to get ready for the wedding—but that was before I learned who they really were. And how grateful I am for that!"

"All right, I'll look into these people and call you back."

"Do it soon," she told him. "I want this story to get out sooner than later."

When she hung up the phone, she couldn't keep the smile off her face. Finally, she felt like she was getting somewhere.

Marty, however, looked horrified. "What did you do?"

"I did what I had to do." She ignored him and walked across the house back to their bedroom and into the master bathroom to start to get ready to go to the sisters' house. She hoped it would be the last time she went there.

Marty followed her. "You called a news station? What happened to just talking it out?"

"Steven wasn't listening." She squeezed toothpaste on her brush and brought it to her mouth. "And you were just going to sit by and let it happen."

"I heard your concerns, but I thought it was just you having a hard time letting him go," Marty said. "Like when he went to college or got his own apartment. You know, normal *growing up* stuff. Not this—I don't believe that you're actually doing this!"

She spit and waved the toothbrush at him. "I'm protecting our son! How do you know we didn't miss a cry for help along the way?"

"Because he's happy! Mary, you've gone through some extremes, but this one—" Marty shook his head and clenched his fists. "I just can't believe that you actually called a news reporter."

"These girls need to be exposed for what they really are." She resumed brushing and looked at herself in the mirror. The bags under her eyes were bad from the rough night, but right now she felt exuberant. Triumphant.

"And what if you're wrong?" Marty asked. "You're going to defame these girls because you don't like them? That's not right."

"And what if they do something bad to our son?"

"First of all, he's an adult," Marty said. "He can handle himself—we didn't raise an idiot. And second, even *if* Samantha was only using him and you had *proof*, you should go to Steven and talk to him like a *rational adult*. Not call the news media because you're not getting your way!"

"My proof is what I saw, Martin." She rinsed her brush and returned it to its holder. She pushed past her husband and went to her dresser, where she pulled out an outfit that would be okay to wear on TV. She was expecting a return call from Eddie Richer any minute.

"I have doubts that you actually saw that," Marty admitted.

Mary pulled on the clothes she had taken out. "Well, watch the news today. Maybe you'll get your proof!"

Marty turned to exit the bedroom. "I'm going to call Samantha and warn her what you've done."

Mary raced after him. "Don't you dare!" She pulled at his arm to stop him. "This was the only choice I had left! If you can't stand beside me and support me, then maybe we need to look at *our* marriage."

He studied her, clenching his jaw and resting his hands on his hips. Mary stared back into his eyes, daring him to push her further. She never thought their relationship would come to this, but here they were.

The intense stare only broke when the phone ring. Mary rushed to answer it.

"Mrs. Harper? This is Eddie Richer. Your story checks out. I have a cameraman who's on his way in. We can meet you at the Walker house. What's the address?"

CHAPTER 19

Samantha stared at the sun's rays attempting to burst through the curtains hanging over her windows. She had just woken up and was taking in the calm before the impending storm of the day. What she knew would eventually be a good storm, but a whirlwind nonetheless.

The peace and quiet of her morning was abruptly interrupted when her body jolted up as Kathy jumped on Steven's side of the bed.

"You're getting married today!" Kathy pounced on Samantha to make sure she was awake.

"If I don't get a concussion before then," Samantha said as she rolled over. "Geez, could a girl have some peace and quiet for a minute?"

"Nope, not today." Kathy rolled off Samantha and lay on her stomach on the other side of the bed. She still had her tank top and shorts on—even when it was twenty degrees outside, the girl just had to show some skin. "We need to relish in the fact that today almost never happened."

"What do you mean?"

"Well, after your officiant was incapacitated, there was almost nobody to even perform the ceremony, which means it never would've happened."

Samantha gave her a look. "We would've found someone."

"That's not what you said last night!"

"I have some clarity in this early-morning light," Samantha said with a smirk.

"You can't just let me have this one victory?"

"You're right. You saved the day. If it wasn't for you, I wouldn't be able to go on living knowing that my big day was ruined by a very real medical tragedy that had absolutely nothing to do with me or my wedding."

Kathy rolled her eyes. "I suppose that's better than nothing, but you don't have to be so smug about it."

"No, seriously, thank you for finding someone else," Samantha said. "Even if he's a little..." She trailed off, but she knew that Kathy got the gist.

"Yeah, but that's not a bad thing, is it?"

"No, but—did you hear anything coming from the spare room last night?" Kathy's bedroom shared a wall with the spare room, so if anyone would've heard anything odd, it would've been her.

"No, was I supposed to?"

"Well, I got up to pee last night and when I came out of the bathroom, Augustus was coming up the stairs."

"He was downstairs?"

Samantha shrugged. "I guess."

"Why?"

"He said he was looking for another bathroom."

"Maybe he was," Kathy said. "We do have another one down there."

"Yeah, it's just, while I was in there, I didn't hear him knock or anything."

"Well, you were half asleep," Kathy said. "And maybe he didn't knock because he took the closed door as a sign that someone was in there."

"But I didn't hear him walk by…" Samantha left out her bigger concern: she still hadn't been able to tap into Augustus's thoughts. Now that she had a handle on her telepathy—at least to drown out all the thoughts—she tried not to eavesdrop on people's thoughts unless she had a reason.

And deciding whether Augustus was trustworthy enough to spend the night and officiate her wedding was her reason, but his mind was like an iron wall. Or maybe she just wasn't that skilled with her mind-reading power yet. It had been a couple months since she'd really used it.

"Stop worrying," Kathy said. "We have a big day. Mary's going to be here in about an hour. The women doing our hair and makeup should be here around the same time. And before all that, we need to get you fed and showered."

Kathy hopped to her feet and waited by the door for Samantha to follow. Allowing herself one last satisfying, joint-popping stretch, Samantha pulled back the covers and got to her feet.

The house creaked and groaned as both sisters descended the stairs and made their way into the kitchen with an extra skip in their step. It was, after all, a big day.

Samantha's buzz of anticipation subsided a little when she saw Augustus on his hands and knees in the kitchen. His staff lay beside him and his head was buried deep in the lower cabinet.

"What are you doing?" Samantha blurted.

He jumped and crashed his head against the top of the cabinet. He pulled himself out—cobwebs clung to his hair—and rose to his feet.

"I saw a rat run by when I came down."

Kathy squealed and brought her arms up close to her chest. Samantha shot her a look.

"I thought I saw it run down there and I was just trying to track it down for you," he went on.

"We don't have rats," Samantha said firmly.

"We did have that family of mice living in the basement a couple months ago," Kathy admitted.

"We got rid of those."

"Maybe more got in and then made their way into the house," Kathy offered.

Samantha wasn't buying it. Other than the occasional mouse in the basement, she never saw any mice in the house—let alone rats. But maybe Augustus was right. Maybe there was a rat in the house.

She tucked her hair behind her ears and crossed her arms. "So Augustus, I think it's time you answered some questions about yourself—"

The doorbell rang and cut her off.

"I'll get it," Kathy said as she rushed out of the room. "Mary must be early."

Samantha held off on asking any questions—especially now that Mary had arrived. She hated having to pretend like she was okay with Augustus performing the ceremony and not Talia. When Kathy first presented the idea of Talia performing the ceremony, she had been a total stranger to Samantha. But she spent time to get to know Steven and Samantha before agreeing to do the ceremony at all. Augustus, on the other hand, barely even seemed interested in the wedding.

While they were alone in the kitchen, she focused her power on him and listened intently for anything that might be coming out of his head.

Nothing.

What was he hiding?

"Samantha!" Kathy cried out in a nervous tone.

That broke her concentration and she ran out of the room to investigate what was wrong. She had a bad feeling this day wasn't going to shape up like it was supposed to.

CHAPTER 20

amantha!" Kathy shouted again as she was pushed aside. Mary barged in, followed by a man with a WICU microphone in his hand and another man with a camera propped up on his shoulder.

Samantha came rushing in from the kitchen and her eyes grew wide. Kathy shut the door and retreated back to where her sister stood.

Mary confidently stood in front of the camera and waved her hand back at the sisters.

"These two, Samantha and Kathy Walker, are Satan worshippers!" she declared.

"What!?" Samantha shouted.

The man with the microphone approached and shoved it

toward Samantha. "Miss Walker, do you have any comment about these allegations?"

"Get out of our house!" she said, staring straight at Mary.

"The story's out!" Mary said with a smug smile. "Your little secret is out there for all the world to see now."

"What the hell are you talking about?" Kathy demanded.

"I saw you perform your Satan ritual yesterday," Mary said, then turned her attention back to Samantha. "And I'm sure you're not innocent either. Are you trying to corrupt my boy?"

Kathy gasped as she replayed the events of last night and the camera panned over to her. She held up her hand to shield her face, but the cameraman adjusted.

"So you have nothing to say for yourself?" Mary asked Samantha.

"Mrs. Harper, please," the man with the microphone said.

The camera panned back to Samantha.

"Get that damn thing out of my face!" she bellowed at the camera.

He took a step back and Kathy knew he was getting a wide shot of the house. In a matter of seconds, their home went from a quiet, peaceful morning to one of utter chaos.

The man with the microphone turned back to Samantha. "My name is Eddie Richer from WICU-TV. Mrs. Harper claims that your sister, Kathy Walker, cast a spell that created a man out of thin air. Is there any truth to that allegation?"

Samantha glared at her sister, but didn't say anything.

SORCERER

With the lack of response, Mary erupted. "Of course there's truth! I saw it with my own two eyes!"

From the kitchen, Augustus stepped out and looked around at what was happening.

"That's him! That's the man she conjured!" Mary shouted, her finger extended in Augustus' direction. "He's the one they say is going to marry my son to this devil-woman!"

"Hey!" Samantha called.

Eddie brushed by the sisters and raised the microphone to Augustus. "Sir, Mrs. Harper says that you were conjured out of thin air yesterday at the Belle Valley Fire Department. Can you confirm?"

"Don't say anything," Samantha told him. She turned her attention back to the intruders and waved them back toward the door. "Out! All of you, get the hell out of here before I call the police!"

"A lot of good they'll do you when I find some proof that you two had tainted my son," Mary said. "What kind of animal sacrifice did you do to get him to fall in love with you?" " I didn't have to—" Samantha stopped mid-sentence.

Mary pushed by her and looked up at Augustus. "Are you Satan? Are you who Kathy was calling to last night? Do these women worship you?"

"We don't *worship* anyone!" Samantha snapped.

Augustus roared and spun his staff high above his head. Under his breath, he murmured words that sounded like gibberish, but Kathy was sure they were ancient charms. Dark lightning struck down from the ceiling, confirming the use of his magic.

Wide-eyed, Kathy immediately put up her hands and froze the room. In an instant, the building argument that filled the room suddenly went quiet. "What the hell is going on?"

Samantha crossed her arms and paced back and forth. "I think you're the only one who can answer that. Obviously you weren't as careful as you should've been last night when you cast the spell to bring this guy here." She nodded to Augustus, who stood frozen with the staff above his head. The lightning streaks were frozen as well. "Didn't you make sure you were alone?"

"I did!"

"And did you use your magic any other time where Paranoid Mary could've seen you?"

"No!"

"Then it must've been when you cast the spell to summon Augustus."

Kathy sighed. "That *was* the last time I used my magic."

Samantha tossed up her arms in frustration.

"But I was alone! I'm sure of it!"

"Obviously not!" Samantha pointed to the cameraman. "You know, when I pictured my wedding day, I didn't think to factor in time to panic over the end of our lives!"

"Sam, I'm sorry! She must've walked in when I was casting the spell and I wasn't even thinking."

"Well, this is what we get for your knee-jerk reaction to our problem," Samantha spat.

Kathy took the insult because she knew what kind of stress Samantha was under. Plus, she also felt like she deserved it. They had always been so careful with magic and literally overnight, all of that was ruined. On possibly the worst day for it to happen.

"What are we going to do?" Kathy asked in a small voice.

Samantha stood with her hands on her hips and looked from Mary to the camera to Augustus then finally back to her younger sister. She let out a deep breath and forced herself to talk in an calm tone, even when all she wanted to do was scream.

"Okay, unfreeze just Augustus and get him out of here," Samantha said. "No good will come from further exposing our magic."

"Well, wasn't the start of that caught on camera anyway?" Kathy asked. "I mean, he's kind of mid-spell here."

"Let's just hope that's not enough to feed a news cycle," Samantha said. "While you're gone, I'll deal with these guys."

"What are you going to tell them?" Kathy asked.

"What I've been saying since they got here—to get the hell out. We don't have to talk to them and they certainly can't be in our house without our permission."

"They didn't seem to listen to you before," Kathy said. "Are you going to use your persuasion to get them to leave this time?"

"No. Finding out about our magic brought them here. I'm not about use it again to get them to leave. That'll only fuel the fire. I'll just have to remind them that they're trespassing and we could sue them for invasion of privacy. I'm sure a news company would love that reputation."

"Good luck."

"Now go, before they all unfreeze."

Kathy nodded and turned to Augustus. With a flick of her hand, he unfroze. When her magic was reversed, he resumed twirling his staff above his head as if he had never stopped.

"Whoa, whoa!" Kathy called out and reached for him to put down his arms. "Easy there. I froze you—and them." She gestured behind her at the people who were still under the effects of her magic. "The danger is put off for now."

Augustus looked curiously at Mary, Eddie, and the cameraman.

"It's okay," Kathy said. "Samantha's going to take care of them. Why don't you and I go in the kitchen and stay quiet, huh?"

Augustus still looked confused, but he turned and followed Kathy out of the room. The sisters exchanged one final glance before they turned out of sight.

Kathy knew that Mary would pick up on the fact that she and Augustus had disappeared in what she would view as a split second. That would only fan the flames on this whole mess, but for the moment, getting them out of the house so she and Samantha could figure things out was top priority. They could worry about the rest later.

Hopefully.

CHAPTER 21

Kathy ushered Augustus into the kitchen and looked around for a place to hide Augustus. Unless he wanted to squeeze into a cabinet, the only options were the basement or out the back door. Given that her memory of the mice in the basement had recently been brought back to her attention, she looked to the back door. Through the window she could see the fresh layer of snow on the ground.

That wouldn't work either.

"Hmm," she murmured.

"What is it?" Augustus asked.

"We need to hide you somewhere," she said. "Those people out there—they're…well, they are accusing us of bad things."

"Bad things?"

"They saw us use magic and they're trying to expose us." Kathy tried to push away the worry that the cameras would still catch something unusual on film—even if it wasn't explicit use of magic. "And since you're the one they saw me summon, it's better if you—"

"Disappear?"

"Yes!" she said. "The problem is, we don't really have a place to put you until we have the house to ourselves again."

Augustus looked through the window out the back door. "I could go outside."

"But it's so cold out," she said.

"I don't mind." He patted his heavy jacket. "I'm dressed for it."

Kathy took in his fur coat and boots. He did look like someone who was ready to hike in the snow.

She sighed. "It won't be for long."

"Okay."

They stepped to the door and she held it open for him. She hated the idea of sending him into the cold because of a mistake that she had made, but they couldn't risk Augustus further blowing their cover in front of the TV camera. Wherever he came from, he obviously didn't know that magic was supposed to be a secret.

That itself was odd since all magical beings agreed to secrecy, but she pushed the thought from her mind. They had bigger things to worry about.

"If it gets too cold, just tap on the window," she said. "We'll think of something else."

"Okay."

Kathy watched as Augustus walked down the snow-covered back steps. His boots crunched in the frigid snow. Kathy shivered by the door and then closed it, hoping nobody in the front of the house felt the chill of the open door.

Peering through the windows, she watched as Augustus tucked himself against the back wall of the house to squat below the window, making it nearly impossible to see him from the house. Hopefully even if the reporters did push through into the kitchen to search for him, they wouldn't be able to see him.

In the next room she could hear voices as Samantha argued with the news crew, urging them to leave. Kathy turned her attention to the cabinet where they kept their potions. She doubted anything would help them get out of this situation, but she thought maybe one of the labels would jog her memory of something useful.

Truth potions.

Healing potions.

Potions to destroy various demons.

There were at least thirty bottled potions in the cabinet and none of them had anything to do with reversing the effects of exposed magic. The sisters hadn't ever faced this issue before and Kathy hoped they never would again.

In the next room, Samantha let out a loud roar. Kathy slammed the cabinet shut and ran to see what was going on.

CHAPTER 22

When Mary, Eddie, and the cameraman unfroze, they each stopped and stared at where Augustus and Kathy had once stood. One-by-one, they began to look around to see if Kathy and Augustus had moved somewhere else in the room.

"What happened?" Mary asked. "Where did they go?"

"Who?" Samantha asked.

"Don't play dumb!" she fired back. "Your sister! And that devil-man she summoned with your voodoo powers!"

Eddie brushed by Mary and raised the microphone in Samantha's face again. "Miss Walker, how do you explain the sudden disappearance of the two people who were just standing here, one of them being your sister?"

Samantha looked between Eddie, Mary, and the camera. Her frustration was about ready to burst. She thought that she'd be spending the morning of her wedding worrying about making sure everyone showed up on time, not trying to keep nosy reporters out of her house.

"I believe I told you all to leave," Samantha said firmly, yet as calmly as she could.

Eddie took a step back, but tried to ask the question again, "Miss Walker, what—"

"I said get out or I'm calling the police." This time, she let a trickle of her persuasion empower her words. As much as she wanted to avoid the use of magic, it was obvious these people wouldn't leave easily.

To further emphasis her point, she extended her hand toward the door, as if they wouldn't be able to find the way on their own.

Eddie turned to the cameraman and waved his hand at the front of his neck to tell him to stop rolling. He pulled a business card out of his pocket and handed it to Samantha. "Just in case you change your mind."

She took it and crumpled it up in her fist. "Don't wait around for my call."

Eddie gave her one last look before he and the cameraman exited through the front door.

Mary, however, stood where she was.

"I'm asking *you* to leave too," Samantha told her.

"You invited me to get ready for the wedding."

"Well, thanks to you there isn't going to be a wedding today," Samantha said. "Congratulations! You won! Now you get to be the one to break it to your son. I want you to see the disappointment on his face."

"Oh, honey, now that I know what you are, I know you've been pulling the strings all along—controlling him like a puppet. I'm sure whatever emotion he'll display at the news will be at your hands."

"Well, I'm flattered that you think I have such power, but I suppose I'm the only one who knows that Steven is a grown adult and can think for himself," Samantha said. "I don't need to control him. That would be what you're doing right now by throwing out these false accusations in order to cancel the wedding."

Mary laughed. "False accusations? Aw, sweetheart, you haven't even answered the question: where did your sister and that man go? The fact that you refuse to answer that tells me that there *is* something going on and I don't want my son to be a part of it."

Samantha stepped to the phone. "I'm calling the police to have you escorted out of here." At the phone, she thought of something better and dialed in Steven's number. She hoped his phone wasn't among the things he had already packed up.

Mary watched as Samantha dialed. "That was too long of a number! You're not calling 9-1-1. Who are you calling? More of your psychotic friends? Surprised you have any at all."

Samantha pressed the phone against her ear and turned her back to Mary. Finally, on the third ring, Steven picked up.

"Oh, I'm so glad you're there," Samantha said. "Your mother—"

The phone was abruptly pulled away from her face. Samantha turned and watched as Mary brought it to her own mouth and said, "Honey, this woman you say you want to marry is—"

"Give me that!" Samantha snatched the phone back, but Mary held her grip. Together, the two women struggled with the phone while distantly Steven's voice called out to them through the speaker.

Mary released one hand from the phone and instead reached for Samantha's hair and pulled. Crying out as she felt several strands pull away from her scalp, Samantha took advantage of Mary's loose hold on the phone and brought it to her face again.

"Your mother has lost it!" she shouted into the receiver as Mary loosened her hold on Samantha's mane.

"Sam, what's going—"

Steven's voice cut out as Mary ripped the entire phone console away from the wall, snapping the cord in half.

Kathy rushed back into the room. "What's going on in here?"

"I'm not going to let you corrupt my son anymore." Mary

tossed the phone console on the floor.

Samantha's eyes flared and she marched toward Mary. "You'd better hope that I'm not everything you say that I am, because if I was, I would be *cursing* you so that every time you opened your mouth, vomit would come out."

Mary's face contorted with disgust and she covered her mouth with her free hand. She backed away toward the door as Samantha continued to march toward her.

"You can do that?" Mary asked.

Samantha swung open the door, ignoring the rush of heat escaping and the cold air coming in. She pointed toward the street. "Get out now, unless you want to see me try."

"Sam," Kathy said as a warning.

Mary stared at Samantha, sizing her up. With her hands shaking, she rushed out into the cold and down the icy steps. She slipped near the bottom, but regaining her footing and continued the trot to her car.

Samantha sneered at her from the doorway. She kept her eyes on Mary until she drove away. Satisfied that she was finally gone, Samantha turned back into the house and slammed the door shut.

"What did you do?" Kathy asked.

Samantha ran her hands through her hair and sunk to the floor. When Talia collapsed last night, she thought her world was crashing down around her. But now, with this fresh new hell, the tragedy of the night before seemed insignificant.

They were not getting out of this one easily.

CHAPTER 23

From the moment he woke up, Steven had a smile on his face. By the end of the day, Samantha would be his wife. Even though they had a close call the night before, the fact of the matter was that he and Samantha were getting married today.

And he had been waiting for that for a long time.

In the kitchen, Steven poured himself a cup of coffee and looked around his apartment. His big plan for the morning was to finish packing what he could from this apartment. Last night was the last night he would ever spend here again, so the bed could be stripped and the sheets washed before they moved all the furniture out. Likewise, after he packed what he needed for their week-long honeymoon trip to the Pocono Mountains, all of his clothes could be packed up for the move as well.

He knew he'd have to start getting ready by noon to get dressed, down to the hall, and make sure everything was set up the way Samantha wanted it before the wedding started at two. She'd told him to start getting ready by eleven, but he knew he had more time than that. The worst of the planning was over.

Steven downed the rest of his coffee and set the mug in the sink. He would also need to do the dishes before he got ready. Most of those were already packed, but the rest could be added to the boxes.

Just as he turned to head to the bathroom to take care of business, the phone rang. He hoped it wasn't his mother calling again to talk him into canceling the wedding. He did not want to have that argument on the same day he expected to watch his bride walk down the aisle.

"Hello?"

"Oh, I'm so glad you're there," Samantha said breathlessly on the other end. "Your mother—"

Steven pulled the phone away from his ear a little as the sound of a scuffle erupted on the other end. He couldn't quite make out what was happening. He stared at the kitchen floor intently as he listened, trying to picture what was playing out at Samantha's house.

"Honey," Steven's mother's voice rang on the other end. She spoke with that sickly-sweet tone that she used when she was being extra patronizing. "This woman you say you want to marry is—"

"Give me that!" Samantha's voice called from the background on the other end.

"What's going on?" Steven asked. "Mom? Sam? Are you guys okay?"

The worst possibility that he could think of ran through his mind: his mother had gone over to Samantha's to tell her to cancel the wedding since she'd had no luck with him the night before. If nothing else, she was persistent.

Samantha suddenly screamed on the other end like she was being hurt.

Again, he called out, "Sam! What the hell is going on?"

Her voice suddenly came back on the line. "Your mother has lost it!" she shouted into the phone, even more breathless than she was before.

"Sam, what's going on?" Steven asked, but by the end of his sentence, a loud dial tone suddenly rang in his ear.

CHAPTER 24

Cassandra stepped off the bus at her stop at 4th and Cherry and walked down the slushy sidewalk toward Walnut, where Mystic Treasures sat on the corner with her and Talia's apartment above it.

After spending the night in the hospital, Cassandra was exhausted. She'd tried to catch some sleep on the reclining chair in Talia's room, but the incessant beeping from the monitors hooked up to Talia, the chatter from the nurses in the hallway, and the chair that evidently wasn't made for a good night's rest meant that Cassandra was tossing and turning all night.

The fact that she was worrying about Talia didn't help either.

Cassandra couldn't stop thinking about the book that

appeared. The grimoire. Even the name of it sent chills up her spine. She had heard horror stories of other witches completely changing who they were after inadvertently touching the book.

The first touch infected their mind without them even noticing. Then they assumed nothing bad was going to happen because they touched it once, what harm could come from just flipping through the pages and seeing what's there? That would lead them to reading over some dark magic and getting bad ideas about how to use it. And finally, before they knew it, they were using those dark spells without any remorse.

This all went with the fact that they were changing in other ways without even realizing it. Getting moody, short-tempered, and isolating themselves from everyone in their lives. The grimoire acted as a disease, infecting every fiber of their being and it all started with a single touch.

That's why Cassandra decided it was best to keep her distance from the book. Keep it wrapped up and as far away as possible from being tempted by it. All night she worried that she had already accidentally touched it and the infection was beginning.

As she approached the corner of 4th and Walnut, she saw a large man peering in the windows of her shop. He was tall and wide-shouldered, wearing a fur coat and heavy boots. None of that stopped her as she had flashbacks to previous break-in and vandalism attempts, of which she'd been able to handle herself just fine.

"Hey!" she barked and ran to close the distance between them. "We're closed!"

The man looked at her and took a slow step away from the window. "Do you own this shop?"

She pulled out her key and dangled it in front of her. "No, I just have this key for decoration."

He stared at her.

"Yes, I own this shop," she said plainly. "But we're closed. Sorry. You'll have to come back some other time."

"I was hoping to come in and look for something."

Cassandra studied him, trying to determine if she should let him in. Mystic Treasures was in no way a thriving business. They got by with their regular customers, but they also weren't in a position to turn off potentially new customers either.

"What exactly are you looking for?" she asked.

"I'm here for a book."

Her heart began to race. "Which book?"

"Do you question all of your customers before you let them in the door?" he asked.

"I do when they insist on coming in while we're closed," she said, letting her exhaustion cloud her better judgement. They didn't gain new customers by being rude. Still, something didn't feel right. "You'll have to come back when we're open."

Neither of them moved. Cassandra wasn't about to unlock the door to let herself in. She'd turned her back to too many shifty people in the past to make that mistake again.

Mug me once, shame on you. Mug me twice…

The man took a deep breath and nodded slowly, apparently realizing that she wasn't budging. He stepped to the curb and crossed the street to the other side and continued down 4th Street toward downtown.

Cassandra turned and watched him walk off to make sure he was a safe distance away before she let herself into the shop. Once inside, she locked the door behind her and rushed behind the counter without turning on the lights or taking off her coat.

Using the altar cloth—and her winter gloves—she clumsily put the grimoire into a box. It had been sitting open on the counter, where she'd left it the night before when she ran out to Saint Vincent. It was a wonder that creep hadn't seen it when he looked through the window. She had a sinking feeling that the grimoire was the reason he insisted on coming inside.

With the book safely tucked away, Cassandra pulled out the binder containing their customer information. Whenever they put in a special order for a customer, she and Talia recorded their names and phone numbers to call them when their order arrived.

Cassandra skimmed the list of names. Her finger ran down the list of entries as she tried to recall that part of her memory. Finally, one page back, she stopped on the name "Kathy Walker." Looking over just beside her name, she confirmed what Kathy had ordered and remembered the day just last week that she called to tell Kathy her order of solomon's seal flowers and green tealight candles were in.

The ones she needed for the wedding Talia had agreed to officiate. The one that was supposed to be today.

The grimoire showing up on the same day Talia collapsed, less than twenty-four hours before she was about to perform a wedding ceremony? Cassandra didn't believe in coincidences and this seemed like a big one. Kathy might not have any answers, but it was a place to start.

Picking up the phone, Cassandra dialed and watched out the window, hoping the strange man wouldn't return.

CHAPTER 25

Steven dropped the phone back on the cradle and grabbed his keys from where they sat on the counter. He rushed to the door, shoving his bare feet in the closest sneakers he could find and grabbing his coat on the way. It didn't matter that he still had his bathrobe on. Samantha sounded at her wits' end. He wanted to get there to make sure everything was okay.

With his mother he never really knew. She wasn't used to not being in control.

He opened the door and stepped onto the snow-covered porch, feeling his ankles immediately freeze from the snow. He fumbled with his jacket and struggled to put it on over his robe, but the soft materials brushing together only made everything bunch up. With only one arm in, he gave up and reached back and closed the door.

"That's quite the outfit."

Steven turned and saw Robert walking up the sidewalk. His car was parked across the street.

"I think it'll be better for everyone if you and Samantha become one of those couples where she picks out your clothes for you." He smiled to show he was joking, but it faded when Steven didn't return it. "What's the matter?"

"Samantha just called me," Steven said. "She and my mother are bickering already and I want to go over there—"

"To do what?" Robert asked.

"To mediate or something, I don't know."

"Your job for this morning is to come with me," Robert said. "We're going to the gym to get you hyped up before your big day!"

"Rob, I appreciate that, but really, I think I should get over to Samantha's."

"Look, you're the one who said you wanted to make sure you didn't see her the day of the wedding until she was in her dress," Robert said. "You said it'd be bad luck or something like that. Don't start your marriage off on the wrong foot. God knows you're lucky someone even *wants* to marry you." He smiled again, but Steven still didn't return it. "Can we at least go inside and discuss this? It's freezing out here."

Steven nodded and led Robert back into the warm apartment. He could already feel the moisture from the snow seeping through his sneakers and making his feet even colder. Some of his toes had already gone numb.

Inside, Steven kicked off his shoes and hung his coat back on the rack. He stepped behind the counter, just in case the phone rang again.

"If it makes you feel any better, Samantha told me to take you out this morning," Robert told him. "She said if I didn't take you out to do something fun, you'd just sit around and pack all morning—maybe even lose track of time and show up to your own wedding late."

"She told you to come here? When?"

"Last night," he said. "At the hall."

"Oh." Steven was hoping it was this morning. At least that way he could be sure that everything else was still going according to plan. He had been leery about the idea of his mother getting ready with Samantha and Kathy. Her relationship with Samantha was tense, at best, and spending an entire day together didn't seem like the best way to remedy that. The phone call earlier was proof.

"So your mom and Sam are arguing already?" Robert asked from the other side of the counter.

"Sounds like it," Steven said. "I've always been the one to calm them each down. Now that I'm not there—"

"The world is not going to fall apart," Robert said. "Isn't Samantha's sister there? Kathy, right?"

Steven nodded. "Yeah, she's there. But my mom might not

listen to her, either."

"Does she listen to anyone?"

Steven chuckled. "My father. Sometimes."

"Look, if you guys are going to get married, they're going to have a build a bridge and get over it eventually," Robert said. "They're grown adults. They can work it out themselves."

He had a point. Steven wasn't sure what he'd even do when he got there. Was he supposed to play babysitter to them all day when he had his own things to do?

"So you and I are going to take some stress off your shoulders," Robert said. "Go put some workout clothes on, because we're going to the gym!" He added quietly, "And a barber."

"A barber?"

He sighed. "Samantha told me to get you a fresh cut and shave—as if I'm a dog groomer. Although in that outfit..." He looked him up and down.

Steven laughed for the first time since his friend showed up. "All right, all right. I'll go change."

"Good! We'll do a little lifting and then a little primping," Robert said. "We gotta make sure you look good for your big day!"

Steven disappeared into his room and pulled out some clothes to wear. As he changed, he thought about whatever was going on at Samantha's house. Robert was right. Samantha and his mother needed to be able to work it out amongst themselves.

Besides, Kathy was there so she'd be able to keep at least Samantha at bay. And Samantha really was going to be the center of attention today.

He was just relieved that nothing bad came from Augustus spending the night. That had made him nervous, but it sounded like everything was going smoothly on that front.

CHAPTER 26

Kathy crouched down beside her sister. "Samantha, what just happened?"

"Mary has officially lost her mind," Samantha said. "That's what happened."

"You basically just confirmed that we're witches," Kathy said. "I know it was in the heat of the moment but—"

"They already have their proof. Mary saw you last night and she brought in the circus this morning to see Augustus show his magic—speaking of him, where is he?"

Kathy bit back her reaction to the shot at her exposing their magic. "He's outside. He said the cold wouldn't bother him."

Samantha rose to her feet and walked over to the destroyed phone. "He should probably come back in. He's more likely to keep quiet in here than if he's spotted out there." She fussed with the cord, looking at both ends.

"Sam, what are we going to do?"

The older witch gave up on the phone cord and pulled out the drawer from the table where the phone sat. She dug around through the contents until she pulled out another phone jack. It was longer than they needed, but it would still work.

"Well, just as soon as I get this phone working again, I'm going to call Steven and make sure the press isn't bothering him too." Samantha pulled the ends of the broken cord out of the phone and the wall and attached the new one. "Then I'm going to go off on him about his mother and her latest efforts to ruin our wedding, which apparently is working. *And then* I'm going to ask him if he wants to elope to get back at Mary."

Kathy made a face. "You know that's not the reason you want to get married. Don't make it the reason for the wedding, either. Love shouldn't be spiteful."

Samantha let out a deep breath and held one hand on the phone. "Well, she's making it incredibly difficult to be anything other than spiteful." She picked up the phone and dialed Steven's number again. It rang and rang and rang, but nobody picked up. Slamming it back in the cradle, she ran her hands through her hair again and closed her eyes in an effort to focus.

Did Eddie Richers and his cameraman move on to bug Steven? she wondered. *I wish I would've been able to warn him.*

Then it occurred to her where Steven probably was: out with

Robert. Last night she had asked him to take Steven out to make sure he had a good day in the morning. At least someone was.

When she opened her eyes, she didn't see Kathy standing in front of her anymore.

"Where'd you go?"

"In here," Kathy called from the living room.

Samantha stepped over and saw her sister standing in front of the TV with the remote control in her hand. She had on NBC, which was affiliated with the local station, and they were playing *The Chipmunks*. Saturday morning cartoons. Such a separation from their current reality. "What are you doing?"

"You said they already caught our magic on tape—or at least Augustus's," Kathy said. "So it made me wonder if they even got anything useful."

"Why wouldn't they have? They were filming us the whole time they were here. It was like an episode of *Geraldo*." Not her finest hour, but they had more pressing concerns than the public perception of them.

"That's exactly why," Kathy said. "There was so much commotion and yelling and then Augustus and I just disappeared when I froze the room. People are going to claim that it was edited or maybe the producers aren't going to put it on because it doesn't tell the public anything. We were just arguing. That's not the content the local news usually puts out."

Samantha shrugged. At least there was a small glimmer of

hope that they didn't have anything concrete. But if there was thing she knew about reporters, it was that they kept digging until they had some proof.

"You keep an eye on that," Samantha said. "I'm going to try calling Steven again." Maybe he was just in the shower or out getting the morning paper the last time she called.

She walked over to the phone and dialed Steven's apartment for a second time. Once again, it rang and rang and rang. Just as Samantha was about to hang up, the ringing stopped when the line on the other end was picked up.

"Steven, it's me. I'm so glad you picked up," Samantha said. "Listen—"

"I thought I told you to stay away from my son?" Mary said on the other end.

"Are you screening his calls now?"

"I suppose I should, now that I know you're calling him."

"Mary, this is getting old. Let me talk to him."

"No," she said firmly. "Stay away from my son. That includes calling. Goodbye."

"Wait—" Samantha didn't even get the word out before the line went dead. Frustrated that Mary got to him first, Samantha dialed Steven's number again, hoping he would get to the phone first—if Robert hadn't already picked him up for the morning.

The phone continued to ring, unanswered. Samantha pictured Mary standing beside it, laughing to herself that she was winning this war. It was all childish. At least one good thing came of this whole exposure mess: she got to see Mary's true colors.

Chatter erupted near the front door and a moment later, someone knocked. Samantha set the phone back in the cradle and called to her sister, "Who is that?"

"There's a bunch of reporters out front," Kathy said. "Guess the word is spreading."

Samantha went to the living room window and fussed with the curtains, making sure they were completely covered. "It must be a slow news cycle to be staked out in front of our house on a Saturday morning."

"Uh, Sam, they cut into the cartoons."

"Huh?" Samantha turned around and saw an older gentleman being interviewed at a desk. Behind him, there were books stacked on bookshelves with trinkets and other objects to give off the sense of academia. "Who is this guy?"

"A professor at Mercyhurst," Kathy said. "Eddie Richers has been referring to him as an *expert* on more than one occasion."

"An expert on what?"

"Us."

Samantha stood next to her sister and crossed her arms as she watched. At the bottom of the screen, the name "Dr. Paul Ginsberg - Professor of Anthropology - Mercyhurst University" was displayed. The camera panned out so that Eddie Richers, who sat on the opposite side of the desk from Dr. Ginsberg, was visible on the screen.

"Based on the reports that we have seen so far," Eddie asked the professor, "what do you think these women are involved with?"

Dr. Ginsberg rocked his head back and forth. "Well, that's difficult to determine with the information we have so far, but judging from the evidence we have gathered—along with some fairly confident assumptions—it is my belief that the Walker sisters are witches."

CHAPTER 27

Steven took one last look at his freshly styled hair and clean shave before he hopped out of the barber chair.

"Looks great, Mr. Harrison." He placed a five dollar bill in the old man's hand. "Thanks a lot. Samantha will love it."

"Oh, of course." The barber reached for the broom and began collecting Steven's fallen hair into a pile. "First rule of marriage: keep the wife happy."

They laughed politely and Steven stepped toward the front window overlooking State Street. There were only a few people milling about outside in the cold. It was overcast, but with the snow on the ground, Steven still found himself squinting from the light.

Robert stepped up for his turn in the chair. Mr. Harrison

waved the cape out in front of him before securing it around his neck.

"Hey, Mr. Harrison, do you mind if I use your phone to check my messages?" Steven asked. "I just want to make sure everything is going smoothly with the girls."

The truth was, he hadn't stopped thinking about that strange phone call he got from Samantha since he and Robert left for their morning activities. The longer he was gone, the more guilty he felt about having left instead of checking in on them.

"Oh, no problem." Mr. Harrison indicated the counter by the door. The phone sat right beside the register.

"Thanks." Steven turned the phone around and dialed.

After punching in his PIN and waiting a few minutes, a robotic voice declared that he had "no new messages."

"Hmm." Steven hung up the phone and looked outside again as a couple walked by on the sidewalk, hand-in-hand.

If I'm going to be Samantha's husband, I need to step up and make sure that she's safe, Steven thought. *Otherwise, I won't be able to uphold the vows I'm about to take.*

He picked up the phone again and dialed Samantha's house. With each passing ring, he wondered why she wasn't picking up. Then it hit him: *Duh, idiot. She's getting ready for the wedding.*

Setting the phone back in the cradle, he spun it back around to where it sat and plopped down in one of the chairs near the door that served as the waiting area.

"Is everything all right?" Robert asked from the barber chair. Mr. Harrison was still working on his cut before he started on his shave.

Steven rested his chin on his palm. "I don't know."

"Did you try calling Samantha?"

"Yeah. She didn't pick up."

"It's a busy day for the ladies," Mr. Harrison said. "Just wait until you see your bride this afternoon. You'll see why she spent all day getting ready."

"They're probably just so wrapped up with everything that they didn't even hear the phone," Robert said. "Relax. Everything's fine. They'd call if there was another mishap."

Steven shrugged. "That's true. I would just feel better if you take me back to my place when you're done. That way, I can try calling again."

Robert sighed, obviously disappointed. "I guess if that's what you want to do. Samantha told me to keep you occupied all morning, but whatever."

Steven was torn. He wanted to make the most of his wedding day and enjoy everything that had been planned, but he couldn't shake the feeling that something wasn't right.

CHAPTER 28

Kathy stared dumbfounded at the TV as Samantha rushed around the house to close all the curtains. They had officially been called out on local television, which she knew would only be a matter of time before national news networks picked it up. The phone had already been ringing off the hook by reporters from other news sources trying to get a quote for their stories. Kathy was sure there were also several wedding guests calling to find out what was going on.

Meanwhile, Kathy couldn't help but feel crippled by the fact that Dr. Ginsberg further explained his theory and got many of his assumptions correct.

He said nobody knew a lot about the sisters because they kept to themselves in order to keep their personal lives private—true.

That they frequented occult shops, such as Mystic Treasures, in order to supply themselves with herbs, candles, talismans, and other ritual items—also true.

And that they've been practicing their craft for years, careful not to expose themselves for fear of backlash—very true.

Kathy just couldn't see a future in which they recovered from this. How would they be able to keep their secret now that most of Erie was talking about them? And soon it'd be the whole country, if not the world.

"Didn't you say Augustus was outside?" Samantha asked when she came back down the stairs. "We need to bring him in before any reporter catches him in an interview. Not to mention the fact that it's freezing outside."

"Oh! You're right!" That snapped Kathy out of her stupor and she raced to the back door, watching for any reporters lurking through the windows. Samantha had drawn every curtain, so the house was much darker than it had been, further adding to Kathy's feeling of doom and gloom—and guilt.

She opened the back door and looked to the spot under the window where Augustus had hid before. Except, he wasn't there. She looked around the rest of the yard, but didn't see him.

"Augustus?" she called out softly. She didn't want to alert any reporters that they were out back. "Augustus?"

"What's the matter?" Samantha asked from behind her in the kitchen.

"I can't find him." Kathy's eyes searched the yard for tracks, but the only ones she could see led from the back steps down to the spot where she saw Augustus hunker down earlier beneath the window. "I think he magically transported himself somewhere else."

"Well that's just great!" Samantha exclaimed.

Kathy shut the door and returned to the warmth of the house. "I'm sure he just wanted to get away from all of this."

"You don't know that, Kathy. In fact, you don't know anything about this guy. What kind of power does he have? Where does he come from? How come he didn't seem to mind the fact that you summoned him, asked him to do a favor, and then he spent the night here? Doesn't he have a family to get back to? Or, at the very least, a life?"

"I don't know, Sam," Kathy admitted in a small voice. She felt about six inches tall. "I messed up. I'm sorry."

Samantha put her hands on her hips and sighed as she studied her sister. "What did he say he was? A wizard or something?"

"A sorcerer."

"Then that's where we'll start." Samantha turned and marched out of the room.

Kathy followed. "What do you mean? What about all the reporters outside? Or your wedding?"

"The wedding's off." Samantha began to climb the stairs. "I'm sure Steven's heard the news by now. If the phone ever stops ringing, I'm going to try calling him again. If not, his mother will tell him, I'm sure."

"And the reporters?" Kathy followed her into her own bedroom.

Samantha knelt beside Kathy's bed and pulled out *The Art of Magic*. "What about them? The story's out. Word has spread. Other than the fact that they're paralyzing us by keeping us prisoner in our own house, there's nothing else we can do about them but keep them away. What we *can* do is figure out just what Augustus's deal is and where he comes from."

"You think he's bad news?"

"I don't trust him," Samantha said. "And the fact that we don't know anything about him doesn't help any." She set the book on Kathy's bed and began to flip through the pages. "We're about to change that. Let's just hope he doesn't try to use his magic in front of any cameras again."

Kathy hadn't thought about that. Wherever Augustus had gone, it was obvious that he held no loyalties to them. Not that she was too terribly surprised. Samantha was right. They didn't know anything about him. Likewise, he didn't know anything about them, except now he knew their magic was exposed. Why wouldn't he run?

"Here it is." Samantha smoothed out the page that read "Sorcerer."

Kathy sat beside her sister and angled her head so she could read too.

A practitioner of the dark arts, sorcerers prey on the misfortune of others, thriving in the chaos they create. For most sorcerers, their main goal is to achieve unlimited power, which they want to acquire all for themselves. While they may seek the help of others to obtain this power, be warned that the sorcerer will double-cross them.

The important thing to remember about sorcerers is they've never had enough. They're always looking for more power and more ways to spread chaos throughout the world.

"Well, that's just *lovely*," Samantha said when she finished reading.

Kathy bit her bottom lip and chipped off her nail polish with her thumb. It's not like she'd need it for today anyway. "Okay, so I really messed up."

"Yeah, you did." Samantha pointed to a small paragraph beside the entry on sorcerers. "What's this?"

Like witches, sorcerers have a form of magic book called a grimoire. Very powerful and very dangerous, these books should be avoided at all costs. Most are hexed and even the simplest touch could cause paranoia.

"At least he didn't have a book with him," Kathy offered.

"That we know of," Samantha said. "Maybe he had it with him when you summoned him and just didn't notice. He was lurking around down here yesterday, he could've stashed it somewhere for us to accidentally touch and then we'd be paranoid."

"Do you think that's what's going on now?" Kathy asked. "That we're just being paranoid and that our magic hasn't actually been exposed?"

"Like an illusion?"

"Maybe."

"But the book didn't say anything about illusions. It doesn't seem like that'd be within the power of sorcerers."

"Their powers are unlimited," Kathy said. "They're driven by their thirst for power."

"Yeah, and they create chaos in order to get it." Samantha motioned out the front window. "We have the chaos! Now we just need to watch our backs to make sure he doesn't try to kill us to steal our powers."

"Augustus was alone with us all night," Kathy said. "Why do you think he *didn't* kill us when he had the chance?"

Samantha considered this. "Maybe I spooked him when I saw him in the middle of the night. I mean, other than when you froze the room earlier—him included—he hasn't seen the extent of our powers. Maybe he's watching us to see what we're capable of."

"Window shopping?"

"Something like that. I mean, I gave him a pretty stern look when I woke up to pee. Maybe that scared him off."

Kathy rolled her eyes. "Yes, because your *stern look* has been scaring off magical enemies for years."

"You know what I mean! He knew I was watching him, so he wasn't going to strike when I was on alert."

"Maybe."

"I'm more concerned about where we go from here," Samantha said. "The book doesn't mention any way to stop him, so we'll have to come up with our own way and hope it works."

"Well, now we have the time."

Samantha shot her a look—a stern look that really did strike Kathy to her core. "But we don't have the means to stop him. Since *you* summoned him into our lives, we're on his radar. He knows we're witches. He knows we're vulnerable. He's not going to come back here until he's equipped enough to kill us."

"But if this evil magic book does exist and he has one, wouldn't that give him enough power to kill us anyway?" Kathy asked. "I mean, if he really is a powerful sorcerer, then killing two witches who don't know much about him shouldn't be hard. Maybe he's searching for this dark magic book to stop us."

"So you think he agreed to help us as a way to spend more time in Erie to find his book?"

"It would explain why he took off when he had the chance," Kathy said. "And if that's the case, it buys us some time to come up with a way to stop him *before* he gets his hands on that book.

Afterwards, he might be too powerful to stop."

Samantha closed *The Art of Magic*. "True. For all we know, he's after our magic book too. After we're dead, who's going to stop him from taking it? He'd be limiting the knowledge of demonic beings one witch at a time." She stood and started for the door.

"Where are you going?" Kathy pulled the book away from her sister and began to leaf through it.

"To look through the collection of herbs we have," Samantha said. "Maybe I can come up with a potion to limit Augustus's powers—whatever they are."

Downstairs, the phone rang again.

"I swear, if that thing doesn't stop ringing!" Samantha called.

"Should we start answering it and telling them 'no comment'?"

Samantha stormed down the stairs, murmuring to herself.

Kathy got up and followed, knowing Samantha's frustration and disappointment might come out in a way that would only hurt their reputation with the press. By time she reached the bottom of the stairs, Samantha already had the phone pressed to her ear.

"Kathy? Yes, she's here."

Who is it? Kathy mouthed.

Samantha swatted her away. "Whatever you have to say to my sister, you can say to me too. We're not interested in making any official statements for the press." She paused. "Mystic Treasures?"

The shop where Talia worked.

Kathy pulled the phone away from Samantha and pressed it to her own ear. "This is Kathy."

Samantha crossed her arms and glared at Kathy.

"Kathy Walker?" The voice on the other end was a woman's and vaguely familiar.

"Yes, who's this?"

"My name's Cassandra. I own Mystic Treasures with Talia."

"Oh, hi," Kathy said. "I'm sorry about what happened with Talia last night. Is she doing okay?"

"Um…sort of. She's fine. I talked to a nurse who said she's medically okay, but she's still not waking up from her coma—and it's not medically-induced."

"Oh, so is that good?"

Samantha made motions to try to get Kathy to hang up the phone, but Kathy kept turning away from her sister, feeling the cord wrap around her body with each twist.

"Not really," Cassandra said. "I'm actually calling because I wanted to talk to you and your sister about her and what happened."

"Well, I'm not sure we'd be able to offer you much insight," Kathy said. "We don't really know what happened. One minute, we were just talking, setting things up for what was supposed to be the wedding today, then the next minute,

Talia's on the floor and…yeah."

"Supposed to be? You guys aren't getting married today?"

"It was my sister who was supposed to get married," Kathy corrected. "But no, some…things have come up and the wedding is off." It occurred to her that they never made an official announcement to any guests, but if their guests had a TV, they saw the news.

"Oh, I'm sorry."

"It didn't have anything to do with what happened to Talia," Kathy said. "There are other…issues that have come up."

Samantha drew a finger across her neck to tell Kathy to stop talking.

"Well, I was hoping to talk to you anyway," Cassandra went on. "Can I come over? It's not something I'd like to discuss over the phone."

"What about specifically?" Kathy picked up the phone console and carried it further into the foyer, away from Samantha. Luckily, Samantha had just put in the longer phone cord so it stretched into the next room.

"Talia's seizure. I can't really say more. Can I meet you somewhere?"

Kathy used her pinky to pull back the curtain on the window beside the front door and peered out into the sea of reporters swarming their front sidewalk. "At this point, we can't really leave the house without being…followed."

"Followed? Oh."

"Yeah."

"To be honest, I think I'm being followed too," Cassandra admitted.

"What do you mean?"

"Well, there was a man outside my shop this morning when I came back from the hospital."

Kathy shot her sister a look, trying to convey to her that Cassandra was telling her something important. "What man?"

"I don't know who he was."

"Can you describe him?"

"Tall, big, built kind of like a football player—hairy. Looked a little like that Grizzly Adams guy. Actually, maybe even hairier."

Kathy couldn't quite imagine someone hairier than Grizzly Adams, but she pressed on. "Did he have a staff, or something that looked like a walking stick?"

"Yes!"

Turning back to Samantha, Kathy mouthed *Augustus*, but her sister just threw up her hands and shook her head.

"Okay, here's what you're gong to do: you're going to come to our house, but you need to sneak in."

"Sneak in? Why?"

"It's a long story," Kathy said. "Are you driving or taking a cab?"

"Um…a bus?"

"No, take a cab. We'll pay you back when get here. Don't tell anyone who you're going to see. Have them drop you off at the corner of Sunnydale Boulevard and West Grandview Boulevard. After the cab leaves, walk up Grandview toward Upland Drive. About halfway up the block, there's an alley. Take that to the end. You should see a giant oak tree on the other side of the fence at the end. Climb the fence and knock on the back door—make sure nobody from the front yard sees you climbing the fence! Okay?"

"Um…okay," Cassandra said.

"Trust me, Cassandra. This is for your own safety as well. If you're spotted by anyone, take a lap around the block until the coast is clear. Got it?"

"Ye—yeah."

"We'll see you soon, okay?"

"Okay."

"Be safe."

After Kathy hung up the phone, she uncoiled herself from the cord.

"What was that about?" Samantha asked.

"Talia's partner, Cassandra, said she saw a big burly man outside her shop this morning," Kathy explained. "I think it was Augustus. Plus, she wants to come here to talk to us about Talia."

"Here you go again, bringing people into our lives when you don't know enough about them. For all you know, Cassandra could be working with Augustus—or the reporters. Maybe she'll come in here with a wire."

Kathy rolled her eyes. "Get a grip, this is local TV news, not the friggin' CIA. Besides, look at it from Cassandra's perspective: her girlfriend just collapsed and now she's alone. And then when she comes home, she sees a large man peering in her windows? She's scared, Samantha, and she obviously doesn't have a lot of family or friends around if she's calling us for help."

"We have enough going on, Kathy, we don't need to invite someone else's problems into our lives!"

"Regardless of the mess of our lives, we're witches. Our job is to protect people from evil. We might have lost a lot of our freedoms today, but I'm not giving up my responsibilities."

CHAPTER 29

"Thanks for the ride." Steven opened the door and stepped out onto the salt-covered street.

"I'll come in and help you finish packing up." Robert put the car in park and turned it off. "No sense in you being alone on your wedding day."

"Thanks." Steven walked up the porch, which had been cleared of snow. His upstairs neighbor must've shoveled it off. He fumbled with his keys, but when he went to unlock the door, he noticed it was already open.

"Hello?" he called as he stepped in.

The room smelled like a mix of cinnamon and disinfectant. Near the entryway sat three trash bags, all tied off. From the doorway, Steven could see several boxes stacked on the kitchen counters.

"Who's here?" he asked.

Robert walked in slowly behind him, his brow furrowed in confusion.

"Hello?" a woman's voice called from the bathroom. A moment later, his mother emerged from behind the boxes. She had on his bathrobe and held a toilet brush in her hand. "Oh, Steven, there you are! It's about time you showed up."

"Mom, what are you doing?" he asked. "You're supposed to be getting ready for the wedding with Samantha."

Mary looked around the apartment. "I got busy cleaning. Would it kill you to run the vacuum now and then? I know you have one. Your father and I bought it for you for Christmas."

"Mom, the wedding is in, like—" He checked his watch. "—three hours!"

She looked behind Steven. "Robert, dear, thank you so much for driving him home. We'll see you later."

"Oh, I was actually going to stay here until—"

She waved to him. "Bye now! Drive carefully in the snow!"

Steven turned and shrugged at his friend.

Robert nodded. "Okay then. I'll see you later at the hall."

"I'll be there," Steven said.

After Robert left, Mary ran up to Steven and hugged him. His body tensed up, he was very aware of where the toilet brush had been.

"Mom, what's going on?" he asked. "I'm so confused. First,

I got that phone call from Samantha this morning with you shouting in the background, and then—"

She waved it off. "That girl is dramatic."

"And now you're here, cleaning my apartment instead of getting ready for the wedding. What's going on?"

Mary shook her head. "There isn't going to be a wedding, sweetheart."

"What are you talking about?"

"Haven't you heard?"

"Heard what?"

"Oh, honey." She stuck out her bottom lip. "This day has just been horrible. Remember last night when I called you? I was trying to tell you that I saw Kathy do...*something* in the bathroom last night at the hall."

Steven hooked an eyebrow. "Something?"

"At first she was alone, then she chanted something, and next thing I knew, there was a man in the stall with her—that man who she said was going to officiate your wedding!"

Steven's eyes grew wide. He wondered if the girls knew, but judging from the phone call he got from Samantha earlier, their house had been his mother's first stop of the day.

"So naturally I was suspicious," she went on. "I tried talking to you about it, but you wouldn't listen."

"Mom," he said as a warning, as if he could pump the brakes on her story and make it so it never had happened.

Mary ignored him and went on. "I told your father about it

and last night he told me I should do something about it, so I did."

"What did you do?"

"See, last night they were airing this special, about Satan worshipers, and I thought: that's it! That's what those girls are!"

Steven brought both hands behind his head and took several steps back. How could this be happening? He didn't want his mother to finish, but at the same time, he wanted to know everything that had happened.

"After thinking about it all night—and I gave it some serious thought, sweetheart, this was not a decision made in haste. I was thinking about you and your father and everyone involved."

"What did you do?" he asked again.

"Well, this morning a reporter called me back and I told him the whole story."

"A reporter?"

She nodded. "That's right. Eddie Richer from WICU? He's such a nice man, even off-camera. Anyway, so naturally, we went down to Samantha's house and confronted her and—"

"You went to their house with a TV crew?" He turned and began fishing through his boxes for his TV. He lugged it back onto the small entertainment center that he got from Salvation Army when he first moved into the apartment and plugged the TV into the wall.

"Just Eddie and his cameraman," she clarified. "I would hardly call it a *crew*. Samantha and her sister were surprised, of course, but they were *vicious* to me. Threatening me and refusing to answer for themselves."

"Of course! You barged into their house!" Steven played with the rabbit ears until the static began to clear and the picture became crisper.

"I demanded answers! Something you should've done a long time ago!"

The image finally stabilized and Steven felt his knees go weak as he saw the coverage outside of the girls' house. There were several different news stations in the front yard. Not just from Erie, but also from Pittsburgh, Cleveland, Akron, Buffalo.

The screen cut to reporters sitting in the newsroom, where they detailed what they'd learned so far. Dr. Ginsberg from Mercyhurst University calling them witches, flashes of B-roll from Darius Wilcox, CPA—where Samantha worked—and outside of the Millcreek Mall—where Kathy worked.

Steven turned to his mother and pointed to the TV. "You did this?"

For the first time, Mary looked nervous. Uncertain of her actions.

"WICU reporter, Eddie Richer, captured this footage from earlier this morning," the newswoman said from the TV.

The next shot showed Mary pushing past Kathy into the house. Samantha came out of the kitchen and Kathy stood by her side. Eddie tried to get the sisters to answer his questions while Mary pointed her finger and accused the sisters of being Satan worshipers.

Soon Augustus came out and raised his staff as dark lightning filled the room. A second later, he and Kathy were gone—along with the dark lightning—and Samantha had moved over six inches from where she was standing only a moment earlier.

The screen returned to the woman in the newsroom. "WICU can verify that this footage has not been modified in any way and reporter Eddie Richer says that what we see in the video is exactly what happened in real time."

The screen cut to Eddie, standing outside the girls' house. He wore a WICU jacket and hat, but most prominent of all was the smile on his face, knowing that he was onto a story that would make his entire career.

"There are absolutely no special effects added," he promised. "What you see is what we saw. Me and my cameraman, Matt. It was surreal—almost like fireworks, but up close and...different. It's hard to explain. But luckily we got some of it on camera. And the way they just disappeared. It was—I don't know what it was exactly, but it was weird."

Back in the newsroom, the woman said, "So far, requests for comments by the Walker sisters have been ignored. But WICU is still actively pursuing this story and will be back with any new developments."

Steven turned back to his mother for an explanation, but

Mary took on the tone of authority in the room. She pointed to the TV.

"Did you know about this?" she asked. "Did you know that they're witches?"

Steven looked between the TV and his mother, not sure what to say.

CHAPTER 30

Samantha sat on the arm of the chair in the living room, watching Cassandra as she wrapped herself in a blanket. She had just arrived, having followed Kathy's directions and even launched herself over the back fence to avoid the reporters out front. In the background, the TV still played.

"Are you sure I can't make you tea or anything?" Kathy asked when she came back into the room. She had put Cassandra's boots over the heating vent for them to dry.

"No thanks." Cassandra pulled the blanket tighter around herself, further concealing the box she had arrived with. The one she refused to hand over to either of the sisters. "You've both been kind enough to me."

"Well, it's the least we can do after we had you jump a fence to get here." Kathy chuckled to lighten the mood but Cassandra only offered a polite smile.

"Why are there reporters outside?"

"You didn't hear?" Kathy looked to her sister for a reaction, but Samantha sat stoically with her arms crossed.

Cassandra shook her head, then noticed the TV showed the front of the house. She looked to the sisters for further clarification.

"Um…it's kind of a long story," Kathy said. "The short version is that Samantha's future mother-in-law is in the midst of exposing us."

"She might not ever become my mother-in-law at this rate. The secret's already out, as you can see from any news network that's paying attention." Samantha nodded to the box Cassandra clutched protectively. "What is it you've got there?"

Slowly, the newcomer pulled the box away from her blanket cocoon and set it on the coffee table in front of her. "This showed up at the shop last night. Just appeared…magically. I was lucky nobody saw. It's been giving me bad vibes ever since."

"Do you mind?" Kathy started to move toward the box.

Cassandra nodded, but added, "Be careful not to touch it directly. There's an altar cloth in there that I've been using to transport it."

"Where did it come from?" Samantha asked.

Cassandra shrugged. "I don't know. Like I said, it just kind of appeared. Judging by the markings on the cover—and the dark, um, pheromones it's giving off—I'm pretty confident it's demonic."

Kathy carefully opened the box and used the altar cloth inside to set it on the table. Samantha looked down at it and concurred Cassandra's thoughts: definitely demonic.

"Do you think this is the grimoire he's looking for?" Kathy asked her sister.

"Could be."

"Who?" Cassandra looked between the two of them.

"Um…a sorcerer that we…well, *I* summoned," Kathy said. "Kinda sorta accidentally."

Samantha shot her sister a look but didn't say anything. Kathy's actions had been intentional, but her results were unexpected. Everything that could be expected from shotty spellmanship.

"Was he the one who was lurking outside my shop this morning?" Cassandra asked. "That confirmed it for me that this book was bad news. We've had thugs and other people who don't like us or our shop, but this man was different. More threatening almost, without any outright venomous words."

Kathy nodded, fully buying into Cassandra's story.

Samantha, however, was more skeptical. Instead, she pretended to listen and tried to focus her newest power in Cassandra's direction in an effort to pick up any thoughts the new witch had.

Please believe me, Cassandra's voice said in Samantha's head.

SORCERER

You both are my only hope now that Talia's hurt—probably from this book. I have no one else.

"Tell us about Talia," Samantha said suddenly.

Cassandra clammed up and sat up straighter. "What do you want to know?"

"How does her seizure fit into all of this?"

Even Kathy was giving Samantha a confused look, but she only sat and listened for Cassandra's response.

"I don't know, exactly. I just know the book appeared in the shop and then shortly after that, I got the phone call from the hospital that Talia had been admitted. When I got there, one of the nurses told me that she was perfectly fine, but she still…" Cassandra's voice broke and she hunched over and covered her face with her hand as she cried.

Kathy hopped over to the couch and rubbed Cassandra's back. "It's okay, honey. We'll figure this out."

Samantha waited until Cassandra had regained some of her composure before she asked, "So you think Talia's seizure was magically-induced?"

"Yes, and her coma too."

The sisters looked at each other to assess what the other was thinking. Even without reading her mind, Samantha knew Kathy wasn't following Cassandra's train of thought either.

"How do you know that? Do you know Augustus—the sorcerer who was outside your shop?" Kathy handed Cassandra some tissues from the table beside the couch.

Cassandra dabbed at her eyes. "No, he didn't look familiar to me at all."

"So why was he outside your shop?" Samantha asked.

"Maybe he sensed the book was there," Cassandra offered.

Samantha pushed her persuasion toward Cassandra to get her to tell the truth. "Is there any chance Talia might be—?"

"No, absolutely not." Cassandra looked right into Samantha's eyes so she knew she was telling the truth.

Samantha probed her mind for any hint that she was lying.

Talia's a good person. She would never use dark magic…or would she?

"Kathy, can I talk to you over there?" Samantha nodded into the dining room.

"We'll be right back," Kathy said as she got up and followed her sister out of the room. When they were alone, she whispered, "It's sad, isn't it?"

"Is it?" Samantha asked. "Seems like a stretch to me."

"What are you talking about?"

"Kathy, come on. Talia collapses when the book just *happens* to show up at their shop? Who put it there and where did it come from? And if Augustus was at the shop, it means he knew it was there, which means he must've had contact with Talia at some point."

"So now you're hating on Talia too?" Kathy asked. "What happened to her officiating your wedding? You didn't think she was involved with black magic before this."

"Yeah, but this is new evidence that's changed my mind," Samantha said.

Kathy shook her head and peered over into the living room at Cassandra, who was watching the news. "No, I don't think Talia and Cassandra have any sort of involvement with anything demonic. Why would Cassandra bring the book to us if she only wanted to use it to hurt us? And those tears? Those were real."

Samantha crossed her arms. "All I'm saying is, do we really need to be taking on anymore stress when we're already in the midst of several different crises ourselves?"

"And like *I* said, we're still witches. We still have a responsibility to help people who need it. Did you try reading her mind? Are there any red flags that come up?"

"No," Samantha admitted.

"Well, there you go. Besides, if Augustus showed up at her shop, it means he's going after other witches now too. And yes, thanks to me he's our responsibility now. I've already apologized for that. But if he's targeting Cassandra and possibly Talia, that makes their problems our problems."

Samantha sighed heavily, but eventually nodded, ceding to her sister's reasoning.

"Um, guys!" Cassandra called from the living room in a scared tone.

The sisters ran over and looked as Cassandra pointed to the TV. On the screen, Eddie Richers stood across the street from Mystic Treasures.

"As previously reported, Samantha Walker's wedding to Steven Harper was scheduled to take place today," he said. "Now, we have reports that Talia Lawson was hired to officiate the ceremony. Miss Lawson is the co-owner of Mystic Treasures here behind me. It's an occult shop that sells items from herbs and candles to books about performing rituals and spells."

"Has he been to the shop before?" Kathy asked.

Cassandra shrugged. "I don't know. We have our repeat customers, but we also get a lot of one-time shoppers who are really only there to check things out. It could've been someone else at the station who's been there. Oh, her I've seen before." She pointed to the screen.

On the TV, a woman in a puffy winter jacket stood outside her porch and talked into the microphone Eddie held to her mouth. "The owners always seemed a bit off to me. There's rumors that they live an *alternative* lifestyle. But I'm no one to judge. Anyway, the shop just draws all kinds of weird people. The kind who typically keep to themselves. Now I know why."

The camera returned back to Eddie standing across the street from Mystic Treasures. "WICU has confirmed that Talia Lawson suffered a seizure last night and has been taken to Saint Vincent Hospital, where she continues her recov—"

Someone from behind the camera shouted, "Look! It's the guy from the Walker house!"

Across the street, Augustus peered in the window of Mystic Treasures.

"He came back!" Cassandra said, pointing at the screen.

Eddie turned and raced across the street, nearly colliding with an oncoming car as he did. The camera followed shakily while Eddie called out, "Sir! Sir!"

Augustus turned and stared at Eddie as he raced to him. Even through the shaky footage, the witches could see in Augustus's eyes that he considered whether he should run or stay.

"Sir! Do you care to comment about the women who own this shop? Are they like the Walker sisters? Are they witches?"

Instead of a response, Augustus grunted and charged Eddie, as if he were a bull charging its prey. Eddie stumbled backward and watched as Augustus offered a venomous look.

Slowly, Eddie took several steps away from Augustus and turned back to the camera. "We will continue to follow this lead and report back with any new developments. For now, I'm Eddie Richers, reporting live for WICU."

When the screen went back to the newsroom, Kathy told Cassandra, "Looks like you left the shop just in time."

Cassandra shrugged. "I guess."

Kathy turned to Samantha. "And we're running out of time. Augustus is on the move and the reporters are closing in."

CHAPTER 31

I knew they were witches," Steven admitted.

Mary scoffed and turned away, bringing a hand to her mouth and fighting back tears.

"But they're good witches!"

"And what's making you say that?" she asked. "How do you know they didn't hex you with their witchcraft?" Tears rolled down her cheeks.

"Mom, they help people," he said in a softer tone now that he saw her crying. "Witches protect the nonmagical from magical attacks—which is exactly what the sisters have always done!"

"Those women are *devils*!"

His remorse faded. "No, they're good people! They help

everyone, even someone like you, who may very well be the most spiteful person on the planet."

"You're not thinking straight," she said dismissively. "That woman has tricked you into thinking that you love her."

"I do love her!"

"No, your feelings have only been directed by whatever spell they put you under," Mary said. "Don't you see? I'm only trying to protect you."

"You're trying to *control* me! It's what you've been doing my whole life! Samantha tried to show me when we started planning the wedding and you just had to have everything your way."

"She saw me as a threat and she wanted me gone."

"Can you blame her?"

Mary's mouth fell open in shock and she clutched her chest. "Are you choosing her over me?"

"I shouldn't have to choose, but after what you've gone and done—" He waved his hand at the TV. "—you've left me no choice. Do you see all of this hysteria that you created? *This* is why Samantha and Kathy need to keep who they are a secret! People like you are so closed-minded that you can't accept anyone else who's different."

"This is not some personality quirk, Steven. This is dangerous!"

"No, you've made it dangerous for them. This is why they've been so particular about who they share their secret with. And you took full advantage of exploiting them." Steven walked over to reach the phone. He had to talk to Samantha. This was exactly what Samantha had been afraid of when she revealed her secret to him last summer.

Mary held out her arms to block his way. "They've gotten their claws so far into you, you're not even thinking clearly anymore! You're sympathizing with your abusers!"

"They're not abusive!" He stood back and allowed her to stop him from moving for a moment, even though he knew he could easily overpower her. But placing his hands on his mother was a line he didn't think he could ever cross. "They're just trying to live their lives!"

"Then how do you explain what happened to that poor girl last night? You can't tell me that it was sheer coincidence that she collapsed and then suddenly Kathy had a new person to perform the ceremony. They decided Talia wasn't good enough and cursed her. Once she was out, they could bring someone else in—someone you wouldn't be able to object to so close to the wedding."

Steven put his hands on his hips and let out a heavy breath. It was his half-hearted attempt to calm his anger.

"And when I left Samantha's house this morning, she told me she was going to put a curse on me," Mary continued.

Steven wished Samantha hadn't said that, but knew he'd probably do the same in her position. He couldn't imagine the immense amount of stress she was under. "She was just angry."

"She was showing who she really was!"

"You pushed her to become something she isn't!"

"Do we need to get you treatment?" Mary asked. "Have they brainwashed you beyond recovery? They make medications that can—"

"Get out." His tone was even, firm. He wasn't going to allow his mother the satisfaction of knowing that she was getting to him.

"Steven, I'm only trying to help."

"If you only wanted to help, you would've come to me when you saw Kathy use magic instead of call the news stations," he said. "Now get out of my apartment or I'm going to throw you out."

The tears returned to her eyes. "Steven, you're the only one I have left. Your father—he and I got into an argument this morning. I don't think he—"

"Take the fact that everyone abandoned you as a sign that what you did was wrong," he said. "You're not going to win me over with this sob story. You did it to yourself and you hurt people along the way. Now, I'm not going to say this again: get out."

Mary stared at him for a moment. "I don't believe what I did was wrong. I think I needed to expose these…*Satan worshipers* for what they are. And I'm going to the police because I know those girls hexed Talia and that's why she's in the hospital."

"Go!"

With her head held high, Mary turned and walked out the door. Steven followed her out and locked it behind her. At this point, he hoped he never saw her again. She had caused enough damage to his life and the person he cared most about.

With the newfound silence of the apartment—besides the news still playing—Steven went to the phone and dialed Samantha's number.

"Look, we're not interested in giving any interviews," she said harshly when she picked up.

"Sam, it's me."

"Steven?" Her tone softened. "Finally! I'm so relieved to hear your voice, you have no idea."

"I'm sorry I didn't call sooner," he said. "Robert took me out this morning and then when we got back, my mother was here and she told me what she did. How are you guys doing?"

"Well, it's certainly not the happiest day of my life like we had planned, but I suppose it's not too terrible. We're still breathing—for now."

"I'm going to try to get to you," he said.

"No, you're safe at your apart—" She stopped, then added, "Actually, no try to get here. Your mother must've told the reporters about the wedding. They found Talia's shop. It won't be long before they track you down too. I want you here with me before they find you."

"Okay, I'll be there as soon as I can. Do you need anything?"

"Just you," she said. "Please be careful."

"I will. I love you."

"I love you too."

Steven hung up and raced to his room, pulling on a warmer set of clothes. He still stank from the gym, but he didn't have time for a shower. He threw on some deodorant, tossed extra clothes in a bag, and returned to the living room.

"They always seemed like nice girls," an older woman was saying on the screen. Beneath, she was identified as "MRS. KORS - NEIGHBOR."

The clip cut to Cheryl, who had originally been their wedding planner before she dropped them as clients. "They had a unique sense of style. Even their house seemed…off. Different. Strange. It was all very spooky, in a way, I guess. Their house was definitely a place that stuck with you."

Another clip showed, this time of an older man in a sweater vest, standing in front of a chalkboard. The bottom of the screen said his name was Roger Mitchell - Professor at Porreco College. "I had Kathy in one of my English classes last semester. She was a good student, although she did make friends with another student who suddenly dropped out more than halfway through the semester. She kept to herself after that. Now I wonder if she had anything to do with his withdrawal from the class."

So now they were turning to people who only had passing encounters with the girls to give credence to the accusations. Steven knew these people weren't major parts of Samantha and Kathy's lives, but the public would get the impression that they were from their coverage on TV.

Shaking his head, Steven clicked the TV off, grabbed his keys from the counter, and raced out the door. He climbed through the snowdrifts in the driveway to get to his car, which had nearly four inches of snow on it. All-in-all the snow accumulation wasn't too bad for a winter day, but it was never a good thing when in a rush.

He opened the door, started the car, put the defrosters at full blast, and pulled out his snow brush to begin to clear off the snow. After he got the windshield and side windows cleared, he heard tires crunch in the snow on the street. Moments later, there were several people racing up the driveway with microphones and cameras.

"Mr. Harper! Is it true you were set to marry Samantha Walker today?"

"Mr. Harper! What can you tell us about the Walker sisters?"

"Mr. Harper! Do you believe you've ever been under the spell of the Walker sisters?"

Despite his car not being cleared off all the way, Steven escaped inside, shifted into reverse and honked his horn as he barreled down the driveway. Through the cleared side windows, he could see several of the reporters had fallen into the snowbanks to dodge his oncoming vehicle.

He didn't care.

Samantha was right. The reporters found him.

Sorcerer

With snow flying off the back of his car, Steven tore down the street. He only hoped he could get to Samantha's house without incident.

CHAPTER 32

Once Eddie had backed off, Augustus turned back to the shop and peered in the window. The witch had to be in there. She had nowhere else to go.

Lifting his staff, he tapped it against the front window of the shop. Gently at first, then harder when he couldn't see anybody come to let him in.

"Hey buddy," Eddie said from behind him. "Ease up. We're not here to break anything. Just want to get some answers."

Augustus only offered Eddie a passing glance, then turned back to the window and tapped it some more.

Eddie looked back at Matt, his cameraman, and asked, "You getting this?"

Sorcerer

Matt hauled the camera over his shoulder again and began rolling.

Augustus, having grown frustrated that nobody was answering, raised his staff above his head and began twirling it. Under his breath, he muttered ancient charms. Dark lightning formed above him, striking the sidewalk and cracking it. Finally, he shoved his staff toward the window and directed the energy in that direction, causing the lightning to strike the glass. It shattered into a million pieces.

"Hey!" Eddie called to him.

The sorcerer ignored him and stepped inside the shop, pushing aside the displays against the window.

"Why are you breaking into this shop?" Eddie held the microphone out to Augustus. "Are you following orders from the Walker sisters?"

Annoyed at the nuisance, Augustus turned and grabbed Eddie by the collar. The reporter stared into his eyes, terrified. Augustus launched Eddie back onto the sidewalk, where he stumbled and fell, sprawled out among the broken glass.

Meanwhile, Matt continued to film.

Once again, Augustus raised his staff, swirled it over his head while murmuring charms, and directed the dark lightning toward Eddie. His magic struck the reporter, sending his body jolting and jerking violently until he lay still on the cold concrete.

Augustus turned back to the shop to continue searching. He

threw down displays and shelves in his pursuit of the grimoire. He no longer sensed the book's presence, but his first attempt at getting inside might've given the witch enough time to cloak it in her own magic. He had to search anyway, just to be sure.

Behind him, Matt had stopped rolling. The cameraman called to someone else on the street who had come out to watch the commotion and told them to call 9-1-1. He hovered beside his coworker and began chest compressions to keep the blood flowing, hoping that he could be revived.

After several more minutes of searching, Augustus determined the witch had moved the book elsewhere. He stepped through the glass and Matt immediately jumped to his feet and took several steps back.

The two shared a tense look, both wondering what the other was going to do. From down the street, two police cars drove up, squealing their brakes on the salt-laden road. Two officers from each car jumped out and pointed their weapons at Augustus.

The sorcerer looked around as more first responders arrived at the scene. Again, he muttered charms to himself, then lifted his staff several inches off the sidewalk and shoved it down again. A single lightning streak struck the pavement and a moment later, Augustus was gone.

CHAPTER 33

What do you think we should do?" Cassandra's voice broke through the quiet exchange of the sisters.

"The first thing we need to do is get rid of that book." Samantha nodded to the grimoire sitting on the coffee table. "It's obviously what Augustus is looking for and the longer we have it, the more it serves as a magnet for him to track us down and maybe even kill us."

"How do you know he even has the power to kill us?" Cassandra asked. "Or that he wants to?"

"He'll do anything to get his hands on that book," Samantha said. "I'm sure he's killed before for it."

"He's a sorcerer," Kathy explained. "And what our magic book says about sorcerers is that they're always hungry for power. That book is full of power, which must be why he's after it." She turned to her sister. "And if he's not against killing, I'm sure he's been hunting witches and other magical beings for years. That's a lot of power he's probably accumulated. We need to be careful."

"Right, but first we need to get rid of the book, then we can get rid of Augustus," Samantha said.

"Except, we don't know what kind of power Augustus has," Kathy said. "I mean, we've only seen a glimpse of it. Who knows what other tricks he has up his sleeve? For all we know, we can destroy the book, but Augustus might just go back in time and retrieve the book before it was destroyed."

Samantha shook her head. "We've never dealt with time travelers before."

"We've never dealt with sorcerers before, either," Kathy pointed out. "And we have no idea what kind of magical beings he's killed and whose powers he's acquired. We need to be prepared for anything."

"But how do we stop him from going back in time and retrieving the book?" Samantha asked. "Are you saying we should be focusing on him first?"

Kathy shook her head. "No, not exactly. That'd be risky. We don't know what he's capable of right now. He could be unstoppable with the grimoire."

"So what do you think we should do?"

"We'll have to destroy the grimoire from the timeline

completely," Cassandra said.

The sisters looked at her.

"What do you mean?" Kathy asked.

"We need to craft a spell—and power it in a particular way—that eradicates the book completely from history," she explained. "Past, present, and future."

Samantha rubbed her forehead, feeling a headache coming on. "Okay, but if we destroy it from the past, won't that also destroy any memory of it? And if there's no memory of it, Augustus wouldn't necessarily be a threat to us, so we'd have no reason to destroy it. Meaning that the book wouldn't have been destroyed in the first place. Am I even making sense?"

"Almost like the grandfather paradox," Kathy said.

Samantha shot her a look.

"What? I've seen *Back to the Future*," she said. "Can't wait for Part II."

Rolling her eyes, Samantha turned back to Cassandra. "Do you know what I'm saying?"

She nodded. "Yes, but we won't have to worry about that. There are simultaneous timelines operating at once. With each decision we make, there's a timeline that exists where we've made different decisions. So by destroying the book from our timeline, what we're really doing is changing our timeline to a different course. Like taking a different exit on a highway and ending up on another highway."

Samantha narrowed her eyes, trying to grasp the concept. "Okay…"

"So by destroying the grimoire, we're creating a timeline where the grimoire doesn't exist," Cassandra went on. "So if Augustus were to go back in time, he would only be able to do so in whatever timeline he's in. Time travel in general requires a lot of power. It's difficult for one magical being to do it by themselves. They'd need to be incredibly powerful."

"Which we think Augustus is," Kathy said.

"Right, but it's nearly impossible to change timelines once it's been modified," Cassandra explained. "Without the book, Augustus wouldn't be able to do it on his own. Even if he somehow finds a way to do it—with the help of someone else equally as powerful as him—it will give us enough time to stop him before he can do anything."

Samantha turned to Kathy. "Does that all make sense to you?"

She nodded. "Pretty much." She looked back to Cassandra. "How do you know so much about time travel?"

"It's an interest of mine," she said. "I've read a lot of books about the theories, processes, and drawbacks."

"So you're not positive that any of this is even true?" Samantha asked.

Cassandra shrugged. "It's magic. How can we be sure *anything* is true?"

Kathy looked over at her sister. "She's got a point. Besides, we're not time traveling ourselves. We're just destroying the book from our timeline so that it removes the option of time travel completely."

Samantha tucked her hair behind her ears and shook her head. "Do either of you even know how to tackle a spell like that?"

"I think I have some ideas about the wording of the spell," Kathy said.

"We'll need to boost the power of it too," Cassandra added. "I know of some ritual tools that may be able to help us. Unfortunately, all of mine are back at the shop and I don't think we're going to get back there anytime soon with all the attention." Her eyes wandered back to the TV.

"What do you need?" Kathy asked. "Candles? Herbs? Talismans? We've got a bunch of stuff here. Come on, let me show you." She led Cassandra back to the kitchen.

"And what should I be doing?" Samantha called after them, but didn't get a response.

With the relentless news coverage of their house, Samantha turned off the TV. She'd had enough. She collapsed on the couch and looked up at the clock on the wall. It was just after noon. If this day had played out like it was supposed to, she might've been putting on her dress for final modifications and adjustments. Instead, her dress still hung on her closet door upstairs, likely to never be worn.

Was I stupid for thinking I could have a normal wedding? she wondered. *Was that too much to ask? Should I have just settled for being happy with Steven, even if it didn't mean marriage?*

But why shouldn't I be able to get married? It's not like I did anything wrong.

The sudden roar of reporters firing incoherent questions broke into her thoughts. She sat up on the couch and tried to peer through the curtains, but only saw the backs of several reporters' heads.

Shortly after, the front door burst open and the loud burst of questions filled the house for a second.

"Mr. Harper! Are you a witch as well?"

"Mr. Harper! Have you ever worshiped the devil?"

"Mr. Harper! Are you still getting married today?"

Samantha got to her feet when the door slammed shut. Steven rounded the corner and he and Samantha locked eyes.

CHAPTER 34

Samantha ran to him, wrapping her arms tightly around him. She snuggled her face into Steven's neck and when his arms wrapped around her, she felt herself unravel. All the stress of the day unloaded now that he was here and she knew he was safe.

"Aw, honey." He squeezed her tighter as he body shook with sobs. "You're okay." He rubbed her back.

They stood like that for a while, Samantha finding comfort in his arms. The way she knew she would. Still, this expression of emotion came as a surprise to her. She hadn't realized she'd been worrying about so much, but a lot of it had happened in just the few short hours since she woke up.

The ruined wedding.

The exposed magic.

Cassandra's plea for help.

It was a lot of weight heavy on her shoulders and even though Steven didn't fix any of them just by being there, he was still the only person Samantha felt comfortable letting her guard down in front of. She didn't have to be strong for him like she felt she needed to for Kathy, and especially Cassandra.

"Come on, let's sit down." He released her long enough to hold her hand and lead her to the couch. Once he sat, she curled up next to him.

"How is it out there?" Samantha brushed away some of her tears and sniffled.

"It's a madhouse," he said. "The reporters are mostly on the sidewalk, but the street is still basically impassable with all of your neighbors and who knows who else out there snapping pictures of the house."

"Coming here was stupid," she told him, even though she squeezed him tighter.

"It was worth it," he said. "I couldn't just sit at my apartment by myself anymore."

There were so many things she wanted to ask him or tell him, but for now she was content just sitting there with him. As if she had pressed a giant PAUSE button on her life, which was exactly what she needed. It *almost* made up for the fact that their wedding day wasn't going to happen anymore. In the end, all she really wanted was to be with him and now that they were together, she felt a piece of her confidence return.

"Do you want to elope?" she asked suddenly.

He chuckled. "I would love to, but I don't think that's going to be possible."

"Why not?"

"Sam, you can't even walk out your door right now without a posse."

"It'll blow over eventually," she said, even though she didn't believe the words herself. It didn't stop her from wishing they were true. "They'll find other things to talk about."

He sighed. "I wasn't going to tell you this because I didn't want to worry you, but I heard on the radio on the way over here that there's speculation you and Kathy might've been involved in Eddie Richers' death."

"What!" She sat up and looked at him. "Eddie Richers is dead?"

"You didn't know?"

"No!" She reached for the remote and turned on the TV. Just when she wanted to see the news, a commercial was playing instead. Still needed to get those sponsors in!

"It just happened," he said.

"But he was just on the TV at Cassandra's shop with—"

"Who's Cassandra?"

"He was with Augustus!"

"Augustus? What about him?"

"Cassandra is Talia's partner," Samantha explained. "In

business and in…life, I guess. And we just found out—because my sister is *just great* at doing her homework—that Augustus is a sorcerer, which is basically someone who thirsts for power all the time and he possibly even kills to get it."

"So we don't trust Augustus anymore? And since Eddie was at Cassandra's shop, you think he was a witch too? Why would he run with a story exposing you if he was one himself?"

"No, I don't think Eddie knew anything about magic," Samantha said. "Your mother must've told him that we were going to get married today and so he tracked that back to Talia, who owns Mystic Treasures, which is where Kathy first got in touch with her."

Steven nodded, finally making sense of it all. "Ahh. So since Talia was supposed to officiate the wedding and she owns an occult shop, it only further proves their theory that you're witches."

"Right. But Eddie was just at the shop reporting when Augustus walked into the frame, looking into the windows of the shop," Samantha went on. "And Cassandra told us that he wanted to get in there earlier because apparently some evil book showed up at the shop that Cassandra claims they have nothing to do with." She waved toward the grimoire sitting on the coffee table. "The jury's still out about that. Anyway, we think Augustus wants the book and was desperate to get inside."

"So then why kill Eddie?"

Samantha shrugged. "Maybe he was in his way. I don't

know. Like I said, sorcerers apparently aren't opposed to killing to get what they want."

"But in the meantime, the way the public sees this, you are friends with Augustus since he was over at the house this morning—which they have on camera, along with him using magic. And I guess they have Eddie's death on camera too."

"Great."

"But they're turning the tape over to the police since it's too graphic to run on TV," he said. "I'm sure they'll be playing as much as they can, though."

Samantha rubbed her forehead again. Her headache was coming back. "This is all a mess. Do you think maybe it's a sign?"

"Of what?"

"That our relationship is doomed."

Steven took her hands and looked in her eyes. "The only sign I see is a warning: don't let my mother find out you're a witch."

Samantha smirked. "We completely missed that sign."

"Yeah, I saw it in my rearview mirror as he plowed right through it," he joked.

"Seriously, though. Our relationship has mostly been pretty easy. We fit together, we get along, we talk out our problems, we compromise. On paper, we have everything figured out. But ever since we decided to take our relationship to the next level and get married, it's just been so hard. First, I almost lost you to a siren, then I thought we were going to break up when you found out who I am, then the whole thing with the shapeshifter at Halloween, and now this. And let's not forget your mother being a pain in my ass this whole time."

"This is just a hiccup."

"Another one? When are things going to smooth out again? Are they? Or should we just throw in the towel and count what we had as a good experience?"

"You don't mean that."

She looked down and sighed. "No, but it seems like the universe is pushing us in that direction, doesn't it?"

Steven kissed each of Samantha's hands. "Look, I don't believe in the grand design of the universe. I'm not a witch. I can't tell you where exactly we'll be in five years or even a week from now, but I do know this: we love each other. And to me, that's gotten us through all of our other hiccups before, so I don't see why it won't this time."

Samantha smiled.

"I *know* we'll be married someday," he said. "Hopefully very soon."

CHAPTER 35

Kathy marched back into the living room a couple hours later with a smile. "I think we've got it!"

Cassandra followed in tow with a canvas bag slung over her shoulder.

Samantha sat up from where she'd been laying with Steven. "The spell to remove the grimoire or the one to kill Augustus?"

"Maybe both, but definitely the one to get rid of the grimoire." Kathy noticed the TV still playing the news. She took a seat on the edge of the couch and watched. "Have there been anymore updates?"

"Just more lies, assumptions, and half-truths," Samantha said.

"You still have a crowd out in the yard," Steven added.

Kathy twisted around and peered through the curtains. "Ugh, all the snow is packed down. We're going to have a mud pit in the spring."

"We're going to be lucky if we even *see* spring," Samantha said. "Apparently Augustus killed Eddie Richers and from what they've shown on TV, the police are looking at our connection."

"But there *isn't* a connection," Kathy said.

"If anything, there'd be a bigger connection to me since Augustus was lurking outside my shop," Cassandra said. "We've been a target for scrutiny ever since we opened."

"Not just that, but your shop is also where Eddie died," Samantha said. "Augustus broke the window with magic and Eddie was trying to stop him. They showed a short clip of it earlier, just before…you know."

They all turned to the TV as a staff picture of Eddie Richers showed on the screen with an image of flowers around it. "EDWARD JOHN RICHERS - 1960-1989" was displayed below his picture.

"That's horrible." Kathy felt a twang in her heart. Like Samantha said earlier, if it wasn't for her, Augustus wouldn't be in their lives. And if Augustus wasn't in their lives, their magic wouldn't have been exposed. Most importantly, Eddie Richers would still be alive too. How many more people were going to die before they could stop Augustus?

Samantha looked to Cassandra. "With you being here, that's going to put a bigger target on your back. Are you sure you don't want to jump ship while you still can?"

Cassandra shook her head. "No. This is the right thing to do. Without Talia, I have nothing. So I have nothing to lose."

"I'm sorry," Kathy said quietly.

Samantha pressed her lips together as she sighed. "Kathy, this isn't your fault."

"Of course it is!" she said. "I was sloppy and summoned Augustus without double-checking the spell to make sure it would bring someone good."

"You were only trying to help," Samantha offered.

"And look where that's gotten us! I'm so sorry for ruining your special day. For both of you."

Steven looked up at her and offered a tight smile. Samantha stared at the floor.

"While I was upstairs, I also tried to come up with a spell to help clear up the exposure, but I don't think it'll work," Kathy said. "I don't think anything will work. We're stuck like this forever."

"We'll figure something out," Samantha said.

Kathy wiped away the few tears that had spilled out of her eyes. "I don't think we will, Sam. And even if we do, your wedding day is still ruined. I can't give you that back."

The room was quiet, except for the news and Kathy's sniffles. It wasn't until Kathy sat down to work on the spells that the weight of her guilt really hit her. It was the first time all day that she'd had time to sit and really think about the mess they were in. No matter how she looked at it, she couldn't see a way out. Even if they could get rid of the grimoire and Augustus, several facts remained: they were exposed; Samantha still wasn't getting married today; and Eddie was still dead.

"Kathy, I'm not mad at you," Samantha said quietly. "You only summoned Augustus to help make sure my wedding still happened. It was Mary who saw you use magic and exploited that. She didn't have to do that."

"But I was sloppy."

"Yes, you were," Samantha admitted. "But you had good intentions. As far as I'm concerned, the only person you exposed us to was Mary. She took it to a whole new level of crazy." She shot a look to Steven. "No offense."

He put up his hands. "Hey, I'm with you guys. My mother was way out of line. She has no idea the trouble she's created for everyone."

Samantha stood and hugged her sister. "Our secret might be out, but they haven't beaten us down yet."

Kathy felt better now that they had acknowledged the elephant in the room. It felt like some of the weight had been lifted off her shoulders—but only slightly. As they said, they still had their fair share of problems. Kathy just no longer felt responsible for them.

"So what's the plan?" Steven asked.

"You're not doing anything." Samantha retook her seat beside him. "You're going to stay here safe and sound."

"I meant, what are you guys going to do?" he clarified.

"Well, I came up with a spell to destroy the grimoire completely from the timeline," Kathy said. "I'm just not sure it'll be enough to do the job."

Cassandra set the canvas bag she was carrying on the floor in front of her. She peered into it as she spoke. "I found some things around here that'll help. You were low on some candles, but I think what we have will do."

"Hopefully," Samantha said.

"I'm worried that these won't be enough, though," Cassandra said.

"Why's that?" Samantha asked.

Cassandra leaned back in her chair. "The grimoire is a powerful tome of magic, even if it is dark magic. If one spell fueled by a couple herbs and candles was enough to destroy it, a witch likely would've done that a long time ago."

"So the spell I wrote it useless?" Kathy asked.

"We need something else to power the spell," she said. "Possibly more witches."

"Three isn't enough?" Samantha asked.

"I don't think so."

"What about Talia?" Kathy asked.

"Isn't she still in a coma?" Samantha asked.

"Yeah, but her magic is still there," Kathy reasoned. "I mean, all we'd need to do is touch her to tap into her energy. It would help fuel the spell, wouldn't it?"

Cassandra nodded. "It could work. Having an extra witch never hurt any spell before."

"But she's in Saint Vincent's, right?" Steven asked. "You're not just going to march in there and cast a spell in front of everyone, are you?"

Samantha shrugged. "The secret's out already. What difference does it make?"

Steven hooked a thumb over his shoulder toward the window. "And how are you going to get there without the nightly news following you to record it all? There'd be no coming back from that."

Kathy twisted around again to look out the window. "Seriously, aren't they getting cold out there? They can't be getting great footage anyway."

"Don't want to miss anything if something happens," Samantha said.

"Which means they're not going anywhere," Cassandra said.

"So you're stuck," Steven added.

"No, we're not." Samantha turned to him with a grin. "I think I have an idea for how to get us out."

CHAPTER 36

With the crowd of reporters lurking outside the witches' house, Augustus kept his distance. He didn't want to draw attention to himself like he did at the witch shop on the other end of town. That had been a disaster and something he barely escaped from. He knew enough to stay away from the flashing lights and to not draw attention to himself more than he already did.

Lurking behind a parked car on the street, Augustus watched the house, waiting for to witches to leave. They would have to eventually. He could be patient. He needed to be if he was going to gain anymore power in order to obtain what was rightfully his.

Augustus had tracked the grimoire down to the witch shop.

The fact that the witch with short hair wouldn't let him in was proof enough that she had it. And yet, when he broke in and went to look for it after she was gone, he no longer sensed the grimoire was there.

Following the draw of power like a dog chasing a scent, the sorcerer had tracked the book down and wound up back at the sisters' house. It was no surprise that all the witches were friends. He just needed to get inside the house and get his hands on the grimoire before they could do anything to stop him. He wasn't sure what kind of power they wielded, but three of them together would make them a formidable force. Augustus preferred to kill his enemies one at a time.

From the back of the house, something caught his eye. Someone with a pink coat walked quickly from the back door to the one lone car parked in the driveway. The engine started and it raced backward onto the street.

The crowd of reporters in front of the house took notice and scrambled to collect their cameras, coats, and other equipment to follow. Lucky for Augustus, he didn't have to waste time by gathering his belongings like the nonmagical did.

Tapping his staff twice on the sidewalk, a streak of lightning shot down from the sky and he disappeared from the spot, only to return in a similar fashion at the end of the block.

Exactly where the car had stopped at the STOP sign.

The figure in the pink coat saw him and quickly raced through the intersection. Meanwhile, Augustus heard several engines start up behind him as the camera crews began to move as well.

Augustus spun his staff above his head and sent a streak of lightning toward the car that was racing away. The attack struck the vehicle, shaking it violently, before it rolled off and came to a stop against a snow bank. Soon after, flames shot up from under the hood.

With another flash of lightning, Augustus was beside the car. He opened the driver-side door and held out his hands, waiting for whatever power the witch had to come to him.

Nothing happened.

The reporters had finally turned around their vehicles and began their chase down the block. Augustus needed to act quick before they caught up to him. He looked closer to make sure the witch was dead, but when he pulled back the hood of the pink coat, he saw a man instead. Certainly dead, but he wasn't a witch.

CHAPTER 37

O kay, he's out of the driveway," Samantha said from the other side of the house.

They were in the backyard, bundled up in boots and heavy winter coats, ready to make their escape. Samantha watched as Steven pulled out of the driveway in her car and one of Kathy's spare coats.

On the other side of the house, Kathy watched for the reporters to clear away from the front yard. Cassandra stood beside her, ready to move at a moment's notice.

"Looks like they're mobilizing," Kathy said. "If we run, we should be able to make it."

"Careful with the ice!" Samantha hopped through the mounds of fresh snow to where Kathy and Cassandra were waiting. There had to be about a foot of accumulation.

"Let's go!" Kathy said.

The trio hobbled through the snow-covered side yard as best they could. They made it to the small snow bank along the curb before a reporter spotted them. He was climbing into the back of a news van.

"Hurry!" Kathy called, pushing through the snowbank into the street. The other witches followed.

Samantha caught the eye of the reporter, but something beyond him made her stop in her tracks. Steven was nearly two blocks away, but at the intersection before that, Augustus stood at the corner, waving his staff above his head. Dark lightning crackled around him as he summoned his magic.

"Sam, we have to go." Kathy grabbed her sister's arm and tugged.

The reporter who spotted them turned to follow Samantha's horrified look. Together they all watched as Augustus's lightning struck Samantha's car. The vehicle bounced up and down on the road before scurrying off and crashing on the side.

"Oh no." Kathy's stomach dropped and she could only imagine what Samantha was feeling. Worse, Kathy knew that even if she had noticed Augustus five minutes sooner, there was nothing she could've done. Her ability to freeze someone in time wouldn't have reached that far.

"Did he just kill one of them?" a reporter up ahead asked out loud.

Kathy shook her head and snapped herself out of her thoughts. She pulled on Samantha's arm, finally getting her into the car. "We have to go now!"

Getting to the hospital to cast the spell with Talia before Augustus or the reporters caught up to them was the only way they could stop the sorcerer from killing more people.

Samantha stared out the back window as Cassandra started up Steven's car and raced down the opposite end of the street. Tears rolled down her face as she erupted in sobs that shook her whole body. Kathy felt helpless as she sat there, rubbing Samantha's back, feeling tears drip down her own face.

Even if they could stop Augustus, it wouldn't bring back Steven. And that was something Kathy knew Samantha would never forgive her for.

CHAPTER 38

Mary stepped into her house and dropped her keys in the dish on the table by the door. She shrugged out of her puffy jacket. The news on the TV echoed from the living room.

Marty must be watching the coverage, she thought to herself.

She knew her home would be tense when she returned, but she was determined to stand her ground and act like everything was normal. Steven had made his point clear—that he had no intention of calling off the wedding. Honestly, if those witches did indeed place any sort of hex on him, Mary didn't stand a chance at breaking it, armed with only words of reasoning.

Her husband, however, could still be convinced that the Walker sisters were bad news. Especially if he'd been paying attention all day and seen everything the news stations had learned and reported.

She walked to the kitchen to make a pot of coffee. It had been a long day and she hadn't slept at all the night before.

"There you are!" Marty called to her.

"Yes, dear, it's me." She placed a new filter in the machine and scooped out the appropriate amount of coffee grounds.

"You've certainly been busy, haven't you?"

Noticing that he was angry, Mary kept her back to him as she filled a mug with water at the sink. She didn't trust herself not to cry if she looked him in the eyes. After the day she'd had, she was worn thin.

"Where have you been?" he demanded. "I've been on the phone all day! Relatives calling in, asking if the wedding is still happening—my sister flew in from Georgia! Oh, and in between fielding calls from confused wedding guests, the phone's been ringing off the hook from reporters wanting to talk to you about possible leads. When they found out I'm Steven's father, they wanted to know *my* side of the story."

Mary forced herself to keep her voice even and calm. "Oh good. I was hoping the guests would know that the wedding was off."

"This isn't a game, Mary!"

Finally, with the coffee machine brewing and nothing left to fuss with, Mary turned and faced her husband. "I know it's not a game, Mart. I've been trying to tell everyone that! Those girls are not good for our son."

"So you don't trust his judgment?"

"I think he's being blinded by lust," she said. "And who knows what else."

Marty rocked his head back and placed both hands on his head. "Do you even *hear* yourself? You think they put some kind of *curse* on him?"

She pointed to the TV. "They had someone from Mercyhurst on there saying that he thinks those girls are witches! And after what I saw last night, I have to believe it. Crazy or not, it's the only explanation that fits."

"And what if you're wrong?"

"I'm not wrong. I'm calling them out for what they are so the whole world knows and my family doesn't get screwed over. I'm doing the right thing."

"Mary, pay attention! You're pushing everyone away with all of this insanity!"

"You and Steven will come around."

Marty put his hands on his hips and shook his head. "Steven will never understand why you're rejecting the woman he loves."

"Consider the alternative, Mart. Let's say we let him marry this devil-woman—this *witch*, as the news said. What happens then? Does Steven become a witch too? Do we just pretend that it's normal? And what if they have children? Will those kids be witches too? Do you want a *witch* as a grandchild?"

"At this point, I really don't care. If pushing him away from us and shoving his life under media scrutiny is the alternative, then yes, I would gladly welcome a witch—or whatever she is—into our family. I only want to see Steven happy."

"So do—"

The TV caught her eye as new footage began to roll. A young woman stood on the street outside the Walker house with her hair pulled back by her earmuffs. At the end of the block, police had taped off an area where a car sat with its front fender against the curb.

"…earlier today," the woman said. "Eyewitnesses say one of the Walker sisters left her house in a pink coat, proceeded down her driveway in her own vehicle, and began heading toward Cherry Street, where she stopped at the intersection with Homeland Boulevard. There, the vehicle was struck down by the man late-reporter Eddie Richers attempted to interview in the Walker sister home this morning."

Mary's heart thundered in her chest. "Late reporter? He's dead?" She looked to her husband, but he kept his eyes glued to the TV.

When Mary looked back at the screen, she saw Augustus, waving that odd staff in the air. Seconds later, dark lightning struck the vehicle, shaking it violently before it rolled off and crashed into a snow bank.

Mary brought her hands to her mouth in surprise. She didn't think all of this attention would lead to one of the sisters dying. But then, they had died at the hands of someone Mary *saw* them conjure. They brought this negative force into their own lives.

Was this the kind of dangers they routinely faced? Did that mean Steven was subject to the same dangers?

The woman on the TV screen touched a gloved hand to her earmuff. "This just in from the newsroom: Erie Police have identified that the driver was *not* one of the Walker sisters, but a young *man* instead."

Mary let out a sudden shriek of horror. If Augustus was the one who killed the person in the car, which belonged to one of the sisters, then that meant the only other man in the car could've been—

The phone rang and she shrieked again.

With a shaking hand, Marty reached for the phone. "He-Hello?" He looked at Mary as he listened. Within seconds, she witnessed raw emotion come over her husband that she ever rarely saw. He clutched the back of the couch for support and bent over. Finally, he said, "Thank you. I'll be down later."

"What is it?" Mary asked, although she feared she already knew the answer. Tears pooled in her eyes. "Who was on the phone? Marty?"

Just as quickly as it came, his turmoil turned into anger. "Our son is dead, Mary. That was the police. They want us to go down and identify the body, but they have a good reason to believe that it's him."

She shook her head as the tears fell. "No—no! They

would've came to us in person if Steven had died. It can't be him!"

"I talked to the police commissioner himself." Marty sucked in his lips, doing his best to keep his voice even. "He said with the media attention and everything that they still don't know about the Walker sisters, they decided a phone call would be the best option to keep us safe."

Mary erupted into sobs and reached for her husband, feeling her knees go weak. Their son—their only child—was dead. The very same person she was trying to protect.

Marty pushed her away and let her sink to the floor. "This is all *your* doing!" He turned and stalked off toward the bedroom.

She watched him leave, then tucked her knees against her chest in an effort to console herself.

What had she done?

CHAPTER 39

The three witches marched through the hospital, ignoring the surprised looks they received from everyone. Samantha and Kathy had been on the news all day, so the fact that they were recognized didn't come as a surprise. Hospital personnel and visitors alike stared at them, some even murmuring, "Is that them?" as they passed.

By time the trio made it to Talia's room, they took solace in the fact that they had a bit of privacy—not that they expected that to last long. One of the nurses would surely be in, likely followed by hospital security to escort them out—maybe even turn them over to the police.

But none of them cared. Certainly not Samantha, who just lost the love of her life, nor Cassandra, whose lover was at risk if they didn't stop Augustus and get rid of the grimoire.

Cassandra went to Talia's side and began explaining what they were doing. Kathy took that opportunity to pull Samantha aside. It was the first moment where they had relative privacy since Steven was killed.

"Are you sure you're okay to do this?" Kathy asked.

"I have no other choice." Samantha looked a mess, but she didn't care. Kathy knew that her sister had compartmentalized her feelings as best she could—putting their task at hand at the forefront of her mind over what she had just lost. Even though it wasn't healthy long-term, there wasn't much else they could do. This was the only window of opportunity they had to get rid of the book—and time was running out.

"If you need a break, let me know." Kathy rubbed her sister's arm, then crossed the room to take the canvas bag from Cassandra.

She set the box that contained the grimoire on the floor beside Talia's hospital bed, then pulled out some other items they had brought with them: three candles, one black, one silver—both to expel negative energy—and one red for defense against black magic.

They would need to create their own altar, so Kathy set the candles on the floor around the grimoire, which Samantha carefully pulled out of the box and dumped onto the floor without touching it directly.

Cassandra rejoined them and began to light the candles.

Meanwhile, Kathy pulled out some herbs to expel negative energy: yarrow flower, wood betony, and witches burr. They had already ground them up back at the house, so now all Kathy had to do was sprinkle them around the makeshift altar.

Beside her, Samantha pulled out the other two remaining herbs. Mullein protected against sorcery and lady slipper protected against hexes and curses. With the arsenal Cassandra had put together, there was no way anything sinister would come within a hundred feet of this place.

The door opened suddenly and a nurse with blonde hair and purple scrubs stepped in.

"Dawn," Cassandra said.

"You know her?" Kathy asked.

The nurse shook her head. "There are too many people in here and—is that an open flame? Put that out!"

"Trust us," Cassandra said. "We just need to do something—" She paused, then restated, "We need to cast a spell or someone bad might come to hurt Talia."

"This is ridiculous." Dawn looked back into the hallway.

"Ignore her," Kathy said. Their lives were screwed anyway, what difference would it make if they performed a spell in front of someone nonmagical? At this point, as long as Augustus was stopped, that would need to be their first priority.

"I'm calling the police," Dawn said. "You can't do this here! This is a hospital!" She left the room. A few other brave onlookers peered through the half-open door.

"Are we ready?" Samantha asked with no emotion.

Kathy pulled the spell out of her jacket pocket. "Candles are lit, herbs are sprinkled around. Now we need to make sure we hold hands with each other, and touch Talia to make sure her magic is factored into the mix as well. Got it?"

Samantha and Cassandra both nodded. Kathy spread out the paper the spell was on, grabbed ahold of Cassandra's hand and reached for Talia with the other. Together, they recited:

Sinister spirits and evil ways,
This tome has far outlived its days.
Summoning the strength of the divine,
Destroy this book from the timeline.

The blast that followed sent the witches flying back in opposite directions, even rocking Talia's bed against the far wall and sending her machines into high-pitched screams.

Kathy's ears were faintly ringing, but she still heard the panicked monitors. She looked to the makeshift altar and saw a small crater in the floor where the book had been sitting.

"Is everyone okay?" Cassandra asked as she sat up.

"Fine," Samantha murmured.

The door swung open and Dawn reappeared. "What just happened in here?" She saw the hole in the ground and looked at each of the witches. "Don't go anywhere." She disappeared back into the hall.

"We need to get out of here." Kathy rose to her feet.

"You guys go ahead," Cassandra said.

"But they'll catch you too," Samantha said.

"I'm going to stay with Talia for as long as I can," she said. "I want to make sure she's safe. Augustus might figure out the book was destroyed here. If he does, my guess is he will want to follow-up on the evidence like he did at our shop. I can't just leave her here."

Kathy was about to protest, but Samantha nodded. "Keep her safe and hold on to her."

Again, Kathy's heart ached for Steven, knowing it was ten-times worse for her sister. But all they could do was move forward. It was what Samantha was doing, even though Kathy knew she wanted to fall apart.

"Be safe," Kathy said. She reached for Samantha's hand and they raced out the door.

CHAPTER 40

The witches' house had been completely ransacked. After they had slipped away, Augustus had transported himself inside. It was partly because he saw the girls sneak out and partly because he wanted to get away from all of the people asking him questions. Funny how they were completely oblivious that he had only transported himself a hundred feet away into the witches' house.

After having torn apart the downstairs in search of the grimoire that he knew had been there at one point, Augustus made his way upstairs. He did a cursory search of the guest room, where he had stayed last night, but wasn't surprised when he couldn't find anything.

He went to the next room, opened up the closets, pulled

back the sheets, flipped over the mattress. He still couldn't find anything. Next, he searched through every drawer in the dresser, moving the whole piece away from the wall to check any other hiding places. As he did, hair products and lotions fell off the top and rolled all over the hardwood floor.

Within minutes, he had torn apart the room and again come up empty. The grimoire was not there. Anger consumed him and kicked the nightstand, knocking the lamp off the top, where it crashed on the floor.

Suddenly, he felt a pang in his chest. The pain was subtle at first, but quickly grew in intensity. He clutched at his chest and fell to the floor, his vision fading to darkness. It was as if his body had suddenly gotten weaker, like he had less energy to even focus, let alone move.

Slowly, the feeling passed. When his vision finally cleared, he realized that he had mostly collapsed on the overturned mattress, which cushioned his head from the hardwood. Even better, he saw something under the bed that caught his eye.

Moving over so he was sitting up straight, he reached underneath the bed and pulled out an old leather-bound book. On the cover was a full moon and the words, "The Art of Magic" emblazoned at the top. It wasn't his family grimoire, but it was the witches' magic book. Everything they had learned about the magical world was within these pages. A sinister smile spread across his face.

Augustus got to his feet and clumsily made his way out of

the room and to the stairs. The grimoire was no longer here, he reasoned. Now he needed to leave with the next-best thing.

Downstairs, he slowly made his way through the mess he created and stopped when something coming from the overturned TV caught his ear.

"Miss Walker! Miss Walker!"

Augustus searched through the rubble and pulled a broken shelf off the top of the set before he straightened the TV. The witches were leaving Saint Vincent Hospital and news reporters were chasing after them on their way to the nearby parking garage.

"Miss Walker! What brings you to Saint Vincent?"

"Miss Walker! Were you here to see Talia Lawson?"

"Miss Walker! Where is the woman you entered with?"

Finally, the older witch stopped and turned to the camera. Her eyes were red and puffy, as was her nose, which Augustus didn't think had anything to do with the cold.

"I do have something to say," she said.

The other witch tugged at her arm, but she shrugged her off.

"My sister and I are not the ones you should be chasing after," she said. "The man you really want—the one who killed Eddie Richers *and* my fiancé—" Her voice cracked and she paused to gain control over her voice. "That man's name is Augustus. He's a sorcerer. My sister and I have no positive connections to him. He's a murderer and a threat and—"

Again, she stopped talking as the tears overcame her.

SORCERER

Augustus, however, felt his blood boil with rage. He knew he had to be careful now that the witches were being reckless with exposure, but to call him out in front of everyone—expose *him* for who he was. That created a whole other level of vengeance that was separate from wanting to get his hands on the grimoire.

He looked down at their magic book in his hands and smiled. At least he had something on them.

When the witch turned back to the camera, she said, "Augustus, I have a message for you: You have taken *everything* away from us, so be prepared because we're coming for you. And we have nothing to lose." She turned and followed her sister toward the parking garage.

The reporters began to fire more questions at her, all talking over one another.

"Miss Walker! What do you mean when you say you're coming for him?"

"Miss Walker! Are you confirming that you're a witch?"

"Miss Walker! Do you have any idea where Augustus might be?"

Augustus shoved the end of his staff straight into the screen of the TV and watched the electricity crackle as it died. His lips curled into a snarl.

That witch thinks she's strong enough to kill me? he thought to himself. He patted the magic book in his arms. *I'm going to have to kill them both with their own magic.*

CHAPTER 41

Neither one of the sisters said anything as Samantha pulled out of the parking garage at Saint Vincent's and raced through the stoplight to turn onto West 26th Street.

For the first time in her whole life, Kathy had no idea what her sister was thinking. She couldn't even begin to imagine the turmoil she was in after losing Steven. It scared her a little to see Samantha so unhinged. Her expression was blank, emotionless, devoid of life.

The impromptu interview she did outside the hospital was further proof that Samantha had given up keeping any of their secrets. It was reckless and purely emotional, which was totally opposite of the way she normally acted.

When Samantha got on I-79 and began heading south,

Kathy finally broke the silence.

"Why were you egging Augustus on?" Her voice was small, but in the absence of the radio or any other conversation, it was almost like she was shouting.

"We have a spell." Samantha kept her eyes on the road, two hands on the wheel. The highway was clear of snow with a whitish hue from the amount of salt that had been sprinkled through the winter.

"But I'm not sure it's even going to work."

"I trust you." For the first time since they got in the car, Samantha looked over at Kathy. "We're all we have left."

Kathy let that statement sink in for a moment. It was the first time it really hit her that they were all alone. Steven was gone and Kathy had no one in her life—the first time in a long time she could say that. They didn't have any other family. Not many friends. Even Cassandra's loyalties were to Talia, which was completely understandable. And now with the media attention, their solitude wasn't likely to change anytime soon.

They were stuck.

"The spell you wrote worked on the grimoire," Samantha said suddenly.

"That was fueled by the herbs and candles Cassandra put together."

"But that stuff wouldn't have helped if the spell wasn't written well," Samantha said. "Besides, you've written spells that have stopped a lot of our enemies in the past. I trust you. Your spell will work on Augustus too."

I would still feel better with a backup plan, Kathy thought to herself. It's not even like they were home—or could stop home—to get the magic book and look through it for any other tips or tricks to help them stop the sorcerer. The person Kathy was still kicking herself for having brought into their lives.

The one who killed Steven, among others.

"Where are you taking us?" Kathy asked.

"Somewhere the reporters will have a harder time finding us. Somewhere Augustus can't hurt anyone else."

CHAPTER 42

Just north of the borough of Edinboro, Samantha pulled into the snow-covered Peninsula Park. Kathy held on to the edge of her seat at the car shook over the unevenly-packed snow and ice. More than once she cringed, worrying that Steven's little car wouldn't make it through the snowbanks, but thankfully it did.

The playground, pavilion, picnic grills, and few benches around the park alluded to a warmer time. The wind coming off of Edinboro Lake had blown most of the snow around and continued to bring the occasional gust that rounded up a flurry of snow into a small cyclone.

Samantha pulled into a gravel parking area that sat only a few feet away from the edge of Edinboro Lake.

"Is this it?" Kathy heard the wind slap against the windows of the car and she shivered. The toasty warmth of the car was more inviting the cold landscape surrounding them.

"Let's go." Samantha turned off the car and got out, leaving the keys in the ignition. She rounded the car and hobbled through the snow, crossing the windblown drifts as she neared the lake.

"Um, Sam!" Kathy got out of the car and chased after her sister.

Samantha softly pressed her toe against the ice where the lake began. After a few more gentle pushes, she shifted her weight on it completely.

"What are you doing?" Kathy asked.

"This was the only place I could think of that was far enough away to lose the reporters and would be remote enough so we don't hurt anyone when we finally get rid of Augustus." She turned and started marching out toward the middle of the lake.

"Sam!" Kathy stopped short when she approached the edge of the lake. Like her sister, she carefully tapped it before deciding she had nothing to worry about. Moving as quickly as she could, she braced herself against the bone-chilling wind and tried to catch up to Samantha. With each step, she feared she was going to break right through and end up in ice cold water.

She tried to convince herself that if Lake Erie could freeze over in the winter, a much smaller lake like the one in Edinboro wouldn't be a problem.

The wind was worse out on the open lake. It was the kind of chill that went right through any number of layers. Kathy pulled her fur-lined hood tighter around her face and buried her other hand deep in her pocket, clutching the spell with her life. The last thing they needed was for the paper to fly away and be left without a way to defeat Augustus.

When Kathy finally caught up with Samantha's power-walking speed, she asked over the roar of the wind, "How are we going to get Augustus out here?"

Before Samantha could respond, a streak of dark lightning struck the ice in front of them and Augustus appeared. Both sisters stumbled backward and Kathy looked around for any sign that the ice was cracking.

Nothing.

The ice was much thicker than she thought.

Augustus didn't seem to be bothered by the weather. He stood with his bare hand on his staff and looked at the witches. "You called?" His lips broke into a sneer.

"You've done enough damage," Samantha said.

Kathy looked from her sister to the sorcerer and noticed something in his free hand. It looked familiar, but in the fading light of the day it was hard for her to place it.

"The exposure of your magic was not my doing," he said. "That would be a result of *your* sloppiness."

"I was supposed to get married today," Samantha said. "And

you *killed* him!" She took a step toward the sorcerer, but Kathy grabbed her arm.

"Sam, wait! He's got our magic book!" Kathy put up her hands to freeze him, but it only lasted a second before he broke free of her magic. "He's too powerful."

Augustus smiled. "Ah, yes, I still have quite a bit of power, even though you've destroyed a family heirloom. No matter, I killed your lover and I stole your book. I think we can call it even."

"I think you can go to hell!"

Kathy pulled her sister closer and lowered her voice. "Sam, we need to get the book away from him. The spell might destroy it and then we'd never find a way out of this mess."

Augustus took advantage of their banter and raised his staff in the air. All around them, the early evening sky lit up with streaks of lightning that struck at different points around the lake. Beyond, the lights in the houses of the borough flickered at the surge of energy.

"We have to do something!" Kathy shouted. She looked over at Samantha, who had her eyes locked on Augustus, seemingly oblivious to everything that was going on around her.

Samantha must've been using her mind specialty, Kathy reasoned.

"I thought you already tried that!" Kathy called to her. She doubted that Samantha would be able to break through his mental defenses. She hadn't been able to read his thoughts last night he was at the house, so what made this time any different? Would the destruction of the grimoire have weakened his defenses?

Augustus seemed locked in a trance as well. The lightning storm around them slowly subsided. He brought his staff down to the ice, but kept his eyes on Samantha.

Kathy braced herself against the wind, wondering what was going on between the two of them in Augustus's mind. She only hoped Samantha was winning. The possibility that one of the powers Augustus had acquired was mind control was a theory she didn't want to entertain.

"Now!" Samantha called out suddenly.

Startled, Kathy asked, "Now what?"

"Grab the book!"

She hesitated, but took a step closer to Augustus, then another. She hoped Samantha's hold on him wouldn't slip while she was right beside him. She pried *The Art of Magic* away from his grip. Clutching it against her chest, she ran back to her sister's side, thankful to put distance between them again.

"Let's do the spell," Samantha said. "I scrambled his mind a little, but I don't know how long it'll take him to unscramble."

Kathy shifted the large book to her other arm and pulled out the paper from her pocket. She huddled beside her sister and read:

DAVID NETH

Powerful sorcerer, evil being,
It is your torment that we are seeing.
For your crimes, you will be punished,
Now that your pull has been diminished.

Disperse your energy,
Set it free.
Your control will no longer be.

Let your reign come to an end,
So our lives can start to mend.
Using the strength of our power,
We make this your final hour!

In a sudden burst, Augustus erupted from the effects of the spell. For the second time that day, Samantha and Kathy were thrown back from the blast of their magic. Both witches skittered across the ice in opposite directions. Kathy, however, managed to keep her hold on their magic book.

With a stiff neck and sore shoulder from landing on the hard ice, she sat up and looked over to where Augustus had been. In his place was a crater—with water protruding from the hole. Worse, Kathy thought she heard the telltale sound of ice cracking.

And they were standing in the middle of the lake.

"Samantha!" she called out and looked over to where her

sister lay on the ice. "Sam, we have to get up!"

With each footstep, Kathy heard more of the ice crack beneath them. The effects of the spell had weakened it and if they didn't get back to land soon, they would be stranded—shocked by the cold water if they fell in. The remoteness of their location that they took to protect everyone in the borough would cost them their lives.

But there was a bigger problem: Samantha wasn't moving.

CHAPTER 43

Sam!" Kathy shouted. Her voice echoed across the vast empty lake. She took off her gloves and tapped both sides of her sister's face. "Sam, come on, wake up! We need to get going before someone comes to check out the blast."

Samantha lay motionless on the ice.

Kathy put her ear close to her sister's face to listen for breathing, but she couldn't hear anything over the wind. And her exposed skin was too numb to even feel for a breath. She wasn't about to open Samantha's jacket and check to see if her chest was moving, so Kathy did the only thing she could think of: she put her gloves back on, set the magic book on her sister's stomach, and came up behind Samantha to drag her back to the car.

It was her only option.

More ice cracked as she dragged her sister to safety. They were concentrating their combined body weight into one area of the ice, allowing the cracks to follow them. Bad move in a situation like this, but there was no other choice.

It wasn't the middle of the lake that scared Kathy so much. It was the edge, where the ice would be undoubtedly thinner, and therefore weaker.

Kathy put that fear out of her mind and focused on getting away from the center of the lake. Each step was a step closer to safety and warmth. Yet each step brought more cracks, which served as a reminder that safety and warmth were not guaranteed.

Finally, they made it to the edge. Kathy looked over her shoulder and navigated around the dormant trees and other brush that separated the frozen water from the frozen ground. Her foot dropped through the ice once, but the water beneath had subsided enough so her foot didn't come back wet.

Moving around the cracked hole, Kathy dragged Samantha up to what she knew was land.

When they were finally back to safety, Kathy collapsed back onto a snow drift, exhausted. Her heart was pounding and she could feel sweat lining her skin under her layers while at the same time her face was numb from the relentless wind.

But at least they were off the ice. The next step was getting Samantha to the car, which felt like it was on the other side of the moon when Kathy glanced over at where it was parked.

With a deep breath, Kathy summoned whatever strength she had left and dragged Samantha the rest of the way to the car, hoisting her up and into the backseat.

Kathy went around to the driver's side, set the magic book on the passenger seat, and started the car. Her frozen fingers immediately went to the temperature controls and blasted the heat.

Climbing in the back seat with Samantha, Kathy pulled off her gloves and rubbed her hands together to warm them up. When she started to regain feeling, she unzipped Samantha's coat and pressed her hand against her chest. Faintly, she felt the soft rise and fall of her breathing and beneath that, the dull pulse from her heart.

Warmer. Samantha needed to get warmer. And to a hospital. Back to Saint Vincent's.

Returning to the driver's seat, Kathy shifted into drive and noticed something in her rearview mirror. Blue flashing lights.

The police.

CHAPTER 44

They had come so close.

The grimoire was destroyed.

Augustus was dead.

And yet their magic was still exposed.

Kathy sat with her back against the cinder-block wall of her holding cell at the Erie Police Department. She was placed in a single cell since she was deemed a high-risk inmate. Whenever she left the room, she had to be handcuffed in case she tried to hurt herself or anyone else.

This day had reached a whole new low.

At least she finally had some peace and quiet away from the chaos of their exposure. Sad that it had to come in a jail cell, but if the day taught Kathy anything, it was that she needed to appreciate even the smallest victories.

It was all she had left now.

Through the bars, she watched the TV mounted to the wall near the ceiling. On the screen, the police went in and out of her beloved family home. The news scroll at the bottom read: MORE OCCULT ITEMS FOUND IN WALKER HOME - POTENTIAL MURDER WEAPONS AMONG THEM.

The only "weapons" the police could claim they found were ceremonial knives or more evidence of previous spells. *The Art of Magic* had already been entered into evidence, likely being read through by someone who didn't understand the world of magic. Someone whose eyes should never have seen a single page of that book.

Back in Edinboro, after Kathy realized she was surrounded by police and without a chance that she'd escape, she was put in handcuffs and questioned in the back seat of a patrol car. Once she made sure they had called for help for Samantha, Kathy kept tight-lipped with any question the officer asked her.

It was much harder to do than she thought it would be, especially as the officer continued to vilify her and her sister. Human nature warranted standing up for yourself. But Kathy refused to say a single thing, knowing it would only ensure her crucifixion.

Maybe she'd be allowed a lawyer at some point, but for now Kathy was more concerned about Samantha, who had been taken to UPMC Hamot down the street from the station.

Apparently Samantha's threat to Augustus on the local news—which was now getting national coverage as well—had sent the police into a frenzy to find them.

Eventually, they were able to track down Steven's car when the sisters made it to Edinboro, and the local police notified the Erie authorities. The police in Erie thought the trip out of town was the sisters' attempt to flee once they had been discovered. And, since they'd been so lucky all day, the police drove through Edinboro just as Samantha and Kathy were casting the spell to kill Augustus. The explosion was on display for everyone.

Which was why Kathy was now sitting in a holding cell waiting to be booked. She guessed the police hadn't figured out what to charge her with yet, but she wondered if they were going to try to go for murder.

"Walker!" the desk officer called to Kathy.

She snapped her head up and looked out into the small corridor. Cassandra stood by the desk where the officer sat.

"You have a visitor," the officer said. "Five minutes."

Cassandra stepped up to the bars of Kathy's cell. "How are you?"

"No touching!" the officer yelled.

Both witches put up their hands to show they were abiding by the rules.

Lowering her voice, Kathy said, "I've been better. What are you doing here? Is Talia okay?"

Cassandra smiled. "She woke up from her coma shortly

after we destroyed the book. The doctors want to keep her for a couple days for observation since they still don't know why she wasn't waking up before."

"Oh, I'm so glad! At least it's better than being out here. I'm so sorry you guys were exposed too."

"Don't be. We're going to fix this. Did you stop Augustus?"

Kathy nodded. "Yeah, but once again, we were spotted and they're probably going to arrest me and Samantha for murder."

"Where is Samantha?"

"She used her mind specialty to keep Augustus at bay while we cast the spell and his magic must've backfired into her mind. And I think the cold got to her too." What Kathy was also afraid of was that her sister was giving up now that Steven had been taken away from her.

"Is she going to be okay?"

Kathy shrugged and smiled to try to cover her tears, but still they fell. "I don't know. I haven't been able to check on her."

"Two minutes!" the officer at the desk said. "Wrap it up, ladies!"

Cassandra turned back to Kathy. "I don't mean to cut talk about your sister short, but since we don't have much time I just wanted to tell you that I think I have a way to fix the exposure."

"You do?" Kathy didn't want to get her hopes up. Their secret was too widespread for it to be contained. And even if they could, Steven was still dead. So was Eddie Richers. Those lives wouldn't be recovered.

"I have a time specialty," Cassandra said.

"Me too!"

"I thought so, based on what I've seen on TV. That clip of you and Augustus disappearing this morning has been playing all day."

Kathy nodded. It was another instance of adding fuel to the already-scorching fire.

"I have a theory: if two witches with a time specialty cast a spell to turn back time, it might be enough power to go back *at least* twenty-four hours."

Kathy's eyes flickered up to the clock on the wall. It was just about seven o'clock. Yesterday at this time they were still setting up for the wedding.

The wedding.

Wow, what a difference a day makes, Kathy thought to herself. *I thought by this time today my biggest complaint would be that my feet were too sore from dancing.*

"That's all I'd need." It'd be enough for her to not summon Augustus, which would prevent the exposure.

Except Talia's collapse. That must've been tied to the grimoire or Augustus somehow. But if the grimoire was destroyed from the timeline completely and they managed to stop Augustus before—

"One minute!"

"I've never turned back time before," Kathy said. "I've only been able to stop it—and only for a little while."

Cassandra nodded. "Me too. But it's worth a try. Two witches are better than one."

"If we go back in time, how will we know not to repeat the events that got us here in the first place?"

"You and I should remember everything, since we're the ones casting the spell," Cassandra explained. "But we'd return to where we were twenty-four hours ago."

"So I'd be at the fire hall, but nobody else will know."

"Right. But turning back time means that Augustus will still be alive," Cassandra said.

"What about the grimoire?"

She shook her head. "It's been destroyed from the timeline."

Kathy was still confused about how it all worked, but she saw the officer get up from her seat.

"Time's up, ladies!"

"Do you have a spell?" Kathy asked quickly.

Cassandra grabbed Kathy's hands through the bars. "Just repeat after me."

"No touching!" The officer came up behind Cassandra and tried to pull her away, but the witches held tight.

We've messed up and paid a cost,
With secrets out and lives lost.
Turn back time, one whole day,
Let us forge a new way!

SORCERER

They repeated the spell three more times. Behind Cassandra, the officer turned into her radio and called for help. Just as the doors burst open and more officers rushed in, they froze, then stepped backwards. Time spend up in reverse and Kathy witnessed all of the events of the day, only backwards.

Finally, the spell's effects slowed, then stopped when she stood alone in the bathroom stall at the Belle Valley Fire Hall.

CHAPTER 45

Kathy looked down at herself and saw the same clothes she had been wearing the day before. She raised her fist in triumph and did a quick, silent happy dance in the small space.

When she was done cheering, she opened the stall door and nearly collided with Mary Harper.

"What were you doing?" she asked.

Kathy only felt a little self-conscious because she was so happy the spell had worked. "Um…I have a song stuck in my head."

Mary cocked an eyebrow, but let the comment pass and moved to the other stall in the small bathroom.

Kathy stepped into the corridor and back into the hall

where Samantha, Steven, Marty, Robert, and even Talia were all there setting up for the wedding.

"Talia!" she cried out and rushed over to hug her.

"Um…hi," Talia said.

Kathy looked over and saw her future brother-in-law. "Steven!" She ran over to hug him too.

"Kathy, what the hell are you doing?" Samantha asked.

She pulled away and looked around at everyone staring at her. "Oh. Sorry. I, uh—I've…I've got nothing to explain that."

Samantha gave her sister a lingering look, then turned back to straighten one of the centerpieces.

Kathy jumped in and began helping them finish setting up the hall as well. The room was a little tense, but not as bad as Kathy knew it could get. Samantha was stressed about the wedding and Mary's side comments about what looked good were annoying, but for the most part Samantha let it slide. After all, the biggest crisis when it came to the wedding had been avoided: Talia didn't go to the hospital for any magical ailments.

While Kathy celebrated that achievement, she still worried about why Talia *didn't* have a seizure like she had the first time she'd lived this day. As far as she knew, the only difference was that the grimoire was destroyed, but she still hadn't confirmed that.

Either way, she was too distracted by the wedding and having everyone back to worry about it too much.

Half an hour later, the door opened, bringing in the frigid

winter air. Cassandra stepped through and closed the door behind her.

Everyone looked at her with a curious look.

"Who are you?" Mary asked bluntly.

"Cassie?" Talia said. "What's going on?"

Kathy grabbed her coat from the hook by the door. She had been watching the door since the spell brought her back. Like they had discussed at the police station, the grimoire might've been gone, but Augustus wasn't.

"She's here for me." Kathy pulled on her coat. "Sam, you want to come out with us? It'll only take a few minutes. You too, Talia."

Samantha and Talia exchanged looks, but didn't argue.

"Samantha's kind of leading the show here," Mary protested. "You're just going to leave us?"

"It's tables and centerpieces, Mary," Kathy said. "I'm sure you can figure it out by yourself. We'll be back in like ten minutes, max."

Her eyes met Steven's and she wiggled her fingers, hoping he understood that that meant it was witch-related.

Outside in the night cold, Samantha and Talia followed Kathy and Cassandra as they led them around the back of the fire hall.

"Do one of you want to explain what's going on?" Samantha asked as they marched through the snow.

"It's a long story," Kathy said. "Basically, there's this sorcerer we need to defeat before he hurts anyone. We have a spell, I think." Ever since she came back, she'd been trying to remember the spell she came up with to destroy Augustus.

"And how do you know this sorcerer is bad?" Talia asked.

"In an alternate timeline—" Cassandra started, but Kathy held out her hand to stop her.

"Not now. I'll explain everything later, Sam. Maybe. After we cast this spell, the only thing I want you thinking about is getting married."

By time they made it to the back of the property near the hedgerow lining Mill Creek, Kathy looked around. Across the parking lot, Norcross Road had full view of what they were doing. The only cover they had was the darkness. The last thing they needed was to be exposed again. But better to do it before Augustus could expose them himself.

"Could we just get this over with?" Samantha whined. "I'm freezing."

"Yeah, I'm not dressed for this weather." Talia shivered. Her bare legs beneath her dress were already an angry red.

"Okay, yeah this'll have to be good enough." Kathy turned her back to Norcross Road and everyone else followed suit. "We need a spell to get him here." She looked to Cassandra. "Can you think of one?"

"Uh, sure. Hold on."

Samantha groaned, but they ignored it.

Finally, Cassandra said, "I think I've got it."

DAVID NETH

In another time you were defeated,
Where your evil ways became heated.
So here in the present, we call you here,
So none of your reign will ever appear.

In a flash of light, Augustus appeared in front of them, holding his staff in his hand. He looked around, confused. It made Kathy smile to confirm that he didn't remember anything from the alternate timeline either.

"Ready?" Samantha asked. "Who has the spell?"

"Repeat after me," Kathy said.

Powerful sorcerer, evil being,
It is your power that we are depleting.

Disperse your energy,
Set it free.
Your control will no longer be.

Using the strength of our power,
We make this your final hour!

Just like before, the blast sent the witches falling back into the snow. Only now, they simply fell into the snowbank and laughed as they picked themselves back up.

"I wasn't expecting that!" Talia said with a smile on her face.

"It packs a punch," Kathy said with a grin.

"Is he gone?" Samantha asked.

"Looks like it." Cassandra walked over to where Augustus once stood. Where the snow had melted down to the grass beneath.

"Cool, then I'm going in." Samantha said. "I'm so cold!"

Talia ran off along with her.

Cassandra held back and walked with Kathy back to the hall.

"Are you going to tell your sister everything that happened?" she asked.

"I don't know. Maybe not."

"How come?"

"Well, in that alternate timeline, Mary found out we were witches and exploited it, which caused ripple effects through the Harper family, even pushing into ours," Kathy explained. "If Samantha knew what Mary was capable of—how heartless she could be in the name of protecting her son—it would only create tension between Samantha and Steven. I don't want them to constantly be bickering about what *could* happen. And who knows? Maybe Mary will come around and might actually like Samantha someday."

"After what I saw in the other timeline, I'm not sure if that's ever possible," Cassandra joked.

Kathy laughed. "Maybe not. But they'll have a better shot if

Samantha never knows how ugly it got."

Cassandra shook her head. "You're a good sister."

"I try."

CHAPTER 46

Samantha's entrance during the procession was aided by the flurry of snow that fluttered through the door when she entered. As she walked down the aisle, Kathy didn't fight the grin that spread across her face, seeing how beautiful her sister was. It was even sweeter because of how differently this day could've gone.

Yet Kathy knew that Samantha and Steven were made for each other. Even in all of the turmoil of the alternate timeline, Samantha and Steven still found a way to be together, if only for a little while. They were drawn to each other and destined to be married. Kathy was sure that the alternate timeline they had escaped from was the only one that ever existed where Samantha and Steven didn't get married.

"Steven, we first met at a time in my life when I felt most alone and like I didn't have anything figured out," Samantha said during her vows. "From the very beginning, you've been my friend, my support, and my partner. You've been there for me while I figured out who I was and what I wanted to do. And although we've gone through a lot, and I'm sure we'll go through a lot more, I look forward to spending the rest of my life with you, forever my partner in crime."

When Talia turned it over to Steven to begin his vows, he immediately started choking up.

"Samantha, you're…a pistol."

The room laughed.

"You're tough and determined, but most importantly loving and sweet. You achieve everything you set out to do, without the possibility of failure even on your mind. You're an inspiration to me and push me to be a better version of myself every day. You're always full of surprises and I can't wait to see what else you surprise me with in the future. I will do everything I can to live up to the title of your husband."

Talia finished the ceremony by proclaiming them husband and wife and telling them to kiss. Samantha and Steven joined hands and made their way back down the aisle for pictures. Kathy hooked her arm with Robert and proceeded down the aisle with them.

The next hour passed by in a blur. The difficult part was over: Samantha and Steven were married. Now it was a matter of making sure the bride and groom got pictures with everyone they wanted.

First up was the whole wedding party, and then Samantha and Kathy took pictures together of the two of them. Samantha had also insisted on Kathy taking pictures with Robert, but after that it was just pictures with various people from Steven's family.

Kathy used her newfound freedom from the responsibilities of maid of honor to grab herself a drink. At the bar, Chip, who was from the fire department, served as the bartender. She was only going to allow herself one drink for the night…or at least until after dinner. She still needed to make her speech with the toast, the words of which had yet to be finalized. She decided to proceed with the same motto she'd always had: Wing it!

"Hey," a deep voice said softly from behind her.

Kathy spun around and was suddenly face-to-face with Jeremy. "Oh, hi!"

He was the last person she expected to see. Especially after the debacle of the alternate timeline, and then preparing for the real wedding, she'd been so swamped with everything that she hadn't thought about much else.

Both Kathy and Jeremy hesitated for a moment before she leaned in and gave him a quick, polite hug.

"I'm surprised to see you here," she said.

He was dressed in a black dress shirt and gray pants, which she thought looked very good on him.

"Yeah, I was debating on whether or not I wanted to come,"

he admitted. "But I've known your sister and Steven for as long as I've known you. I wanted to wish them well on their big day. I wasn't *officially* invited, but I ran into Steven the other day at the liquor store and he said that you still weren't planning on bringing a Plus One, so…"

"So you thought you could still be my date." She laughed. "They didn't mind?"

Jeremy scrunched his face and rubbed the back of his head. "Uh…they don't really know. If you think it'll be a problem, I'll leave."

"No, I think you're fine," Kathy said. "Just don't do something stupid to steal their thunder."

"Yeah," he murmured.

Her smile faded and the energy between them grew awkward again. "So how have you been?"

"Good! I got a job."

"You did? That's awesome! Where?"

"Blue Water Insurance," he said. "It's on State Street. It's paperwork stuff, basically."

Kathy nodded. She'd been in the office for Blue Water Insurance before when she and Samantha were facing the harpies. Absently, she wondered if Jeremy had gotten Mark Gad's old desk.

"What about you?" he asked. "What are you up to?"

"Oh, I'm working too," she said. "At the mall. Just part-time still. And I'm taking classes at Porreco College. Just a couple. I started last semester and the spring semester starts next week."

"Nice, what are you majoring in?"

"Just General Studies right now." It had been almost six months since they'd broken up and Kathy wasn't sure if she was winning the "who did better" tug-of-war that always existed between exes.

He nodded. "Nice."

"Yep." Kathy sipped her drink and looked over to where Samantha and Steven were finishing up their pictures. "Looks like we're going to be sitting down to dinner soon."

"Right. I should get going since I don't exactly have a seat."

She smiled, a mixture of relief and disappointment overcoming her. She wanted him to leave so she could move on with her life, but seeing him reminded her of just how much she missed him.

And seeing Samantha and Steven so happy to be together, Kathy couldn't help but wonder if she and Jeremy had made a mistake by breaking up. Their relationship had always been fun. Sure, they had struggles, but there was definitely chemistry between them. That spark was something she hadn't felt with anyone else since Jeremy.

"Well, it was good seeing you," she said.

"Yeah, you too." He leaned in for another hug and his hand lingered on hers when he pulled away. "I've really missed you, Kathy."

She smiled at him again. "Yeah, I've—I've missed you too."

"I'm really sorry for the way things ended between us," he said.

He was making it hard for her to say goodbye to him again. But she tried to be the strong, reasonable one. "Don't be. You were going through a lot and—listen, it's over, right? That's in the past."

Jeremy studied her, and then he was kissing her. Kathy tensed up, shocked by the gesture, but then leaned into it.

He pulled away from her and looked down at the floor. "Sorry. That was out of line. You're probably seeing someone."

"No, actually, I'm not." She tried to collect herself, but the kiss threw her off her train of thought. "Um…I'm kind of busy here, but Samantha and Steven are going to want some time alone tonight and Steven's apartment is all packed up for him to move in, so I need to find a place to stay…"

Jeremy smiled. "Michael's staying at Maddie's tonight if you're asking."

She debated whether she wanted to go down that road with Jeremy again. Hadn't they already established that they didn't work? Or were their problems only exasperated by the side effects of the siren's magic? Their relationship was worth giving it another shot, even if it was only in the name of fun.

"Well, I still don't have a car, so…"

"I'll pick you up," he said. "Just give me a call and I'll be by. And if you change your mind, there's no hard feelings."

She smiled. "Then okay then. I'll see you later."

Jeremy leaned down and kissed her hand. "I can't wait."

Valentine's Day is right around the corner, but neither Samantha nor Kathy are feeling in the mood lately. Samantha and Steven have been arguing about where to live while Kathy has been awkwardly reuniting with her ex-boyfriend Jeremy, who might also be dating someone else.

Scarlett, an enchantress, tracks Kathy down at work for help saving her lover from an evil witch who put him in a spell that Scarlett is unable to break with her own magic. The witches lean in to the distractions from their personal lives and are ready to travel to Buffalo to help Scarlett reunite with her lover. Except, Steven and Jeremy insist on coming along for the weekend, drudging up all of their issues that they'd rather escape from. Worse, Jeremy still doesn't know that they're witches.

What could go wrong?

Enchantress is the sixth book in the Coven series, which serves as a prequel series to the Under the Moon series.

ENCHANTRESS

COVEN: BOOK 6

Read on for an excerpt of the next book in
the Coven series!

DAVID NETH

CHAPTER 1

- APRIL 1988 -

Scarlett walked through the commotion backstage of Shea's Performing Arts Center where stagehands, technicians, and managers all mingled in an effort to bring in the set pieces of *Me and My Girl* that had just arrived in Buffalo from their stop in Pittsburgh. It was organized chaos as different members of the crew pitched in to help make a new place out of the blank canvas that was the stage.

And what a stage it was! Scarlett's favorite thing whenever they arrived in a new city was walking on stage prior to showtime to get a sense of the place before she stepped out to perform. She loved standing beneath the tall, immaculate ceilings, being the center of attention, even if it was for an audience of none.

"Hey, get out of the way!" one of the stagehands called to Scarlett as they rolled in a large backdrop.

Scarlett took several steps backward and let out a yelp as she reached the edge of the stage.

Before panic could really set in, she felt a strong grip on her arm pull her back to her feet.

"Careful," a young man said with a smile. He wore a navy blue T-shirt and black work pants. Clipped to the top of his side pocket was a silver pocket knife. "You'll learn where the edge is after a few more trips." He released his grip and offered his hand. "I'm Oliver."

"Scarlett." The size of his arms suggested his strength, but she was surprised that his handshake was gentle.

"I know this sound forward, but I just have to say that you are gorgeous."

She could feel the heat rise to her face, especially as their hands remained locked together. "Well, if we're being strictly objective, I would have to say that you're not so bad yourself."

His cheeks turned up into a wider smile. "So why don't we take this from a formal observation to something a little more casual?"

Scarlett pulled her hand away. "Easy there, Oliver. I make it a general rule not to date locals. I'm always traveling on one show or another, which I very much enjoy. I'm never around long enough to make anything last—not to say that I don't have fun." She smirked at him.

He opened his arms. "Hey, maybe I'd be the one to make you stay."

She crossed her arms and looked him up and down, the smirk still present on her face. "You're going to have to try real hard to impress me."

"I never turn down a challenge."

Rolling her eyes, she turned away from him. "I'm going to go back to my hotel and rest up before rehearsals start tomorrow. It was nice meeting you."

"Take it easy, Scarlett," he said. "We'll be seeing more of each other!"

"Until my show rolls out of here at the end of next week."

Around the corner, Scarlett stepped into the rehearsal space and nearly collided with Ella, who played Lady Jackie in the show.

"Scarlett," she said very succinctly, as if her name were a command.

"Sorry, I wasn't paying attention."

"I can see that." Ella nodded back toward the stage where Oliver was moving sacks of sand, the muscles in his arms straining from the effort. "He's cute."

"That he is," Scarlett agreed. "And quite the charmer too."

"Oh, so you were talking to him?"

Scarlett nodded.

"Normally, I'd take that as you having dibs, but I know you have that silly rule about the locals, right?"

Another nod. "Yeah, and that's exactly what I told him."

Ella smoothed out the corners of her bright red lips, then fussed with her blonde hair. "Well, I have no such rule."

Scarlett motioned back toward the stage. "Then by all means, be my guest. But quite frankly, I don't think he'll go for you. He seems to have his eyes locked on me."

Both women looked over as Oliver noticed them watching. He waved and they each returned the gesture before he went back to work.

Ella pursed her lips. "We'll have to see who he chooses."

CHAPTER 2

Kathy zipped up her backpack and hauled it onto her shoulder. She already dreaded the long walk to the bus stop and the ride back to the stop near her house. Her back was nearly aching simply from the idea of lugging all of her books that far.

While she filed out of the classroom with the other students, she focused most of her energy on the discussion from class on American Literature during the Civil War, specifically Harriet Beecher Stowe. The crowd in the hallway didn't even register on her mind until she heard a familiar voice call her name.

"Kathy!"

Whipping her head around, she found herself face-to-face with Jeremy.

"Oh! I didn't even see you!"

He chuckled. "I called your name a few times."

"How did you know I would be here?"

"You told me you had class today, and Porreco College isn't that big," he said with a shrug. "Didn't take me long to find which one was yours."

"So you stalked me." She adjusted the strap on her shoulder.

"When you put it like that it sounds creepy. Here, let me take that."

Before she could protest, he pulled her bag off of her shoulders and lifted it onto his, which was an odd look for someone in a button-down shirt with a tie.

"Thanks." She looked him up and down. "You look nice. Did you just come from work?"

He nodded. "I thought maybe the two of us could go to dinner. I made reservations for five-thirty."

Kathy checked her watch. It was just after five and her stomach growled.

"Sounds like you're hungry."

She smiled. "I mean, I've gotta eat sometime."

"Then let's go." He started leading her down the hall toward the exit. "I found this great place in the city. Total neighborhood restaurant, great Italian food. You'll love it."

Kathy followed him out to his car and climbed in the passenger seat, just as if they'd never taken that six-month break. It was natural, spending time with Jeremy again. It was nice and familiar. She missed him.

They had reconnected at Samantha and Steven's wedding, which brought back a rush of emotions that got the better of them. That night they had hooked up for the first time since the breakup, but Kathy was adamant about taking things slow from then on. If they were going to get back together, she wanted to know that things would be different. Dinner was a good start.

The closest parking spot to the restaurant that Jeremy could find was half a block down Plum Street. If it weren't for the bitter temperatures and the chilling wind, Kathy wouldn't have minded the walk. As it was, they didn't say much on their brisk walk until they were inside the warm building.

"Hi, I have a reservation for two at five-thirty," Jeremy said to the hostess.

"Right this way." She led them to the back of the restaurant in a cozy corner.

The walls were adorned with old pictures of the family who owned the restaurant. Shots from throughout the years as the restaurant slowly evolved over time, polaroids from family vacations to Europe or to National Parks out west.

Kathy smiled at the sentiment. It was one of the things she loved about her own house. The history of it was hers and her family's. Nobody could take that away from them. It was nice to see the same pride of place here.

Jeremy and Kathy both scanned the menu in silence. The awkward tension between them built as more time passed. The waitress came over and they each ordered, Jeremy insisting on a beer. Kathy contemplated a beverage herself, but figured it was best to keep a level head during this conversation. Besides, when she got home she'd have to work on homework.

"So how's school?" Jeremy asked after the waitress left their table.

"Um…not bad." Kathy rubbed the back of her neck, then ran her fingers through her hair.

"But not great?"

"Well…"

"I'm surprised you're doing the whole college thing," he said. "I never thought you were interested."

She shrugged. "I mean, that's kind of always been the plan."

"Yeah, but that's always been Samantha's plan. Not necessarily yours."

"True, but what she says makes sense. I'll have a better shot of getting a better-paying job with a college degree."

"What do you think you want to do when you're done?"

The waitress came over and set a tall glass in front of him. He offered her a quick thanks and then reached for it to take a sip.

"I'm not sure yet," Kathy admitted. "I still haven't decided on a major."

"How long are they going to let you take classes without a major?"

"I don't know, but I took an English class last semester and

I liked it. I'm taking another one now and it's good. Maybe I can do something with that."

"With an English degree? What are you going to do, teach?"

She made a face. "I don't think I'm cut out to be a teacher."

Jeremy chuckled. "Then what are you going to do with that degree?"

"I don't know, Jeremy," she snapped. She turned her attention to the photos on the walls. One was a black and white photo of a group of kids standing beside a garden hose. Judging by their clothing, it looked to be a hot summer day.

He pushed his glass aside and leaned forward. "Sorry. Didn't mean to push any buttons. I just—I thought I would offer realistic scenarios."

"I know, but it's something that I'm constantly worried about. I want to start pulling my weight with the bills and everything so the sooner I figure out what I'm going to do, the better."

"That's fair," he said. "But you don't want to lose yourself in the process. Kathy, what I like most about you is that you don't care what other people think. You've always done your own thing."

She smiled. "Thanks. Anyway. So how's your new job? Where is it again? Blue Water Insurance?"

He nodded. "Yeah."

"How do you like it?"

"It pays well enough."

"But you don't *like* it…" She pinched her straw and leaned forward to take in a sip. "A bit like the pot calling the kettle black here, isn't it?"

That brought a grin to his face. "Touché. No, it's not terrible. It's similar to what I went to school for, but not quite. It's a stepping stone."

Kathy nodded. "Gotcha."

A stepping stone job was far from her reach. She was stuck jumping from one low-rung job to the next. But, like Jeremy said, until Samantha's nagging made her feel like that wasn't good enough, Kathy had been happy with all the other aspects of her life. And she always managed to get by when it came to money.

Jeremy studied the photos hanging on the wall while Kathy twirled her straw in her ice water. Apparently after covering their bases with their jobs, they had run out of things to talk about. That thought made her a bit sad.

Was there relationship that shallow before? She didn't think so, but then, they were always doing something the first time they dated. Going here or there, or seeing this person or that. There was rarely any time with just the two of them to sit down and talk. But whenever she needed someone to lean on, Jeremy had usually been there. It was that glimmer of hope that she clung to now.

"I suppose the awkward silence was inevitable," she joked.

He offered a polite smile. "There's a lot for us to catch up on.

Sounds like we've both changed a lot."

And yet the passion between us is still burning bright. Kathy thought back to the night of Samantha's wedding and her cheeks flushed a little.

After another few empty seconds passed, she decided to brave the question. "So what exactly are we doing?"

"You mean about us?"

"Yeah. We had that one-night stand, which I thought was great. But then we've been fumbling around each other ever since. It's been almost three weeks. When are we actually going to talk about it?"

Jeremy let out a heavy breath—clearly a ploy to buy time. He glanced toward the door and immediately stiffened up. Facing forward again, he kept his head low.

"What is it?"

She looked toward the door herself, but didn't see anyone at first. She scanned the room and her eyes landed on the woman sitting at the bar in a beautiful black dress. She was nursing a glass of wine and casually flipping through a magazine.

Kathy turned back to Jeremy, suddenly annoyed that an innocent woman minding her own business intruded into their dinner so completely.

"So do you want to tell me who that is?"

CHAPTER 3

"Surprise!" Steven said with a big smile as he shifted the car in park.

Samantha looked out at all the monochromatic townhouses surrounding several small parking lots jutting off the winding road that seemed like a maze. It was just off one of the arterial roads out of the city, and directly across from Porreco College.

Nervously, she climbed out of the car. "What is this? I thought we were going to dinner?"

"We will. This is just a little detour."

From the nearest building, a man stepped out and zipped up his black puffy winter jacket. He grimaced in the cold, but plastered on a smile when he saw Steven, waving the hand that held a clipboard. "You must be the Harpers!"

Steven stepped forward and the two men greeted each other like old buddies.

"I'm Stuart Jemson, the property manager for Willowood Village." He turned to Samantha. "And you must be the new Mrs. Harper!"

Despite the ambush, being called by her new name brought a smile to Samantha's face and she shook Stuart's hand to be polite.

Stuart clapped his hands along his clipboard. "All right, we're taking a look at a three bedroom, two-and-a-half bath today. It's just across the way here, so we won't be in the cold too long."

He led them across to a nondescript building and let them in the door to the unit on the right.

There was plastic over the carpeting to give the impression that everything was newly-installed, but Samantha could see a few stains on the edges of the room, outlining where the previous tenets had had their furniture. Worse, the room had an odd smell, like fresh paint and cigarettes fused together.

Samantha felt her stomach go queasy and she brought her gloved hand to her nose for a moment to make sure she could hold down her lunch.

"This is one of our largest units," Stuart said. "There are three levels: the walk-out basement, the ground floor here, and a second story above. There are balconies on this level and the one below us. Upstairs, there's a master suite with a walk-in closet…"

Stuart continued talking as Samantha wandered throughout the apartment. It wasn't terrible, if she was being honest. It certainly needed to be aired out, but she knew several people who lived in apartments like these and loved it. The problem was, it wasn't her style.

Worse, Samantha thought that Steven had given up on the notion of the two of them getting their own place. To her, it didn't make sense to move out when she and Kathy already had a huge house—one that they owned free and clear.

This whole apartment tour came as a complete shock because Steven hadn't mentioned much about moving out since they really began planning their wedding. Guess it was something they hadn't ever discussed.

"The second bedroom upstairs is right next door to the master, making it a perfect place for the two of you to expand your family," Stuart went on.

Steven nodded. "Sounds great!"

"We also have several playgrounds on the property, so all the kids can play and the families get to know each other," he went on. "It's a real, true community."

But not my neighborhood, Samantha thought. She had always envisioned her kids would play in the same yard that she and Kathy had. That they'd draw sidewalk chalk on the steps where they passed out candy at Halloween or waited for the school bus. Samantha wanted the traditional idea of community, not the cardboard box version.

"And for both kids and adults, we have a community pool, which is perfect in the summertime," Stuart added.

Steven nudged Samantha's arm. "You always said you could use a pool when it's hot out. Now we have one!"

She gave a tight smile.

Apparently picking up on his wife's mood, Steven turned to Stuart and said, "Would you mind if we checked out the second floor on our own? I think we'd like to discuss some things between the two of us."

"Oh sure!" Stuart leaned against the counter in the kitchen. "You go right ahead and take all the time you need! I'll be right here when you're done!"

Steven smiled and led Samantha upstairs. They stepped into the nearest bedroom, a small one that overlooked the communal backyard, and Steven closed the door.

"So what do you think?"

Samantha raised her eyebrows, an argument about being blindsided on the tip of her tongue. "It's…it's kind of *bland.*"

Steven looked around at the pearly-white walls. "Looks like a clean slate, or a fresh start. Kind of like our marriage, right?" He wrapped his arms around her and they looked out the back window.

She squirmed in his grasp. "I'm not used to a clean slate. I'm used to living in my family's history—the place where I grew up."

"You just haven't lived anywhere else. Trust me, I thought it'd be weird when my parents sold the house that I grew up in—and it was for a little bit, but I adjusted. Things change, Sam. It doesn't mean it has to be bad."

"I know, but…" *But what about Kathy?* she thought. That point would not strengthen her argument for keeping their living arrangements the same. "I just can't picture myself living in this type of *community*."

"It's just a start," he said. "And think about the location. It's easy to get to everything—and right across from Kathy's school! She could stop by anytime."

Knowing that that offer would be short-lived, Samantha decided to side-step it instead.

"It's more than that, though. Where are the trees? Where's the neighborhood character?"

"It's with the people," Steven said. "We'll just have to get to know our new neighbors."

"In the community pool, where everyone's probably peed? I would seriously question that water."

"So avoid the pool."

"And like you said, Kathy's college is right across the street. It's still a new school and they don't have any dorms or anything. Soon this family-friendly neighborhood will be full of college kids partying at all hours of the night. If we start a family, I don't want our kids around that."

"So we'll move by time it gets that bad."

Samantha made a face and looked around the small room again. She could picture a crib and some toys in the corner, but in her head they were someone else's. Not hers. "I don't know, Steven."

He huffed. "Fine. I'll go tell Stuart to forget the whole thing. I just thought *I* would bring an option to the table for a change." Turning, he crossed the small hallway to the stairs and left her standing alone.

TO READ THE REST OF **ENCHANTRESS,**
ORDER YOUR COPY AT
DAVIDNETHBOOKS.COM/COVEN

MORE BY THE AUTHOR

To find more books by the author, visit
DavidNethBooks.com/Books

* * *

Subscribe to his newsletter to be the first to know of new
releases and special deals!
DavidNethBooks.com/Newsletter

* * *

**If you enjoyed the book, please consider leaving a
review on Goodreads or the retailer you bought it from.**
Reviews help potential readers determine whether
they'll enjoy a book, so any comments on what you
thought of the story would be very helpful!

ABOUT THE AUTHOR

David Neth is the author of the Coven series, the Under the Moon series, Heat series, the Fuse series, and other stories. He lives in Batavia, NY, where he dreams of a successful publishing career and opening his own bookstore.

Also writes small town romance as D. Allen.

www.DavidNethBooks.com

www.facebook.com/DavidNethBooks